I0667455

SALON TALK

Topic of Discussion

Men-Tal

Library of Congress Control Number: 2011923450

ISBN 13: 978-0-9843426-9-3
       10: 0-9843426-9-9

Cover Design: Maurice Ingram and Men-Tal

Published by G Publishing, LLC

Printed in the United States of America

Acknowledgments

I would like to thank the Most High for blessing me with the gift of vision and determination which allowed me to put this beautiful work together. I would like to especially thank my family my Mother, Evelynn Lusk, my Father Melvin Christian Sr. My Daughter Tiarra Christian, My Son Melvin Christian 111, My sister's Marketta Lusk, Marletta Lusk, and my baby sis Jesica Christian. My brother's Marcus Lusk 111, Andre Jones, Brian Christian, and Montel Morton (The Champ). It's my honor to thank my Goddess Ms. Chantelle R. White, you are a phenomenal black woman fulfilling your dream of owning and directing your Phlebotomy (GTP) School which is timeless. I'd like to thank my cousin Mr. Maurice Ingram for always putting in the time to help me produce top notch quality graphic designs for my book covers, Joann Ingram aka Truth to Real, your music is the antidote to heal our damaged communities and world, Dolorous Christian, Larry Carter (L.C) Darlene White, Ms. Hatti Pitts (Nana) Richard Pitts, and Tony Quick. I also would like to thank Mr. Darius Blackmon for providing captivating photography and astounding concepts for my book cover, Ms. Venus Davidson (My main character, Cognac) Martina Jennings (Makeup artist, and stylist) Ms. Que, Ms. Teaira McCoy, Ms. Aalysis "BELOVED" Appleseed (My Editor), Ms. Julia Hunter (My Publisher). I want to thank my readers Darius Keaton, Karm`es (May) Houser, and Nneka Dorsey for help keeping my work tight. I want to thank Jerry Krebs for that motivating quote "People don't fail they just quit trying" I'd like to acknowledge a very young talented brotha Mr. Sky Chatman for releasing his first novel (Deceitfully Yours) you have now etched your name in history. I know your parents Ira and Delaine Dixon are proud of you. Thanks and much appreciation to all the book clubs, and everyone who bought my last novel "SPIT", yes the sequel is definitely in the making. Congratulations to Alicia Marion and John George for building the beautiful JAVA House for everyone to come to and enjoy over at the Artist Village. Peace to all my Poetry Fam. And last but not least.........Big ups to my poetry collective "Black Ink" A conglomerate of Fiyah Spittin Poets I am honored to be a part of over the last decade. Keep bringing the flames, INK and HONOR!!!!!(Salute)

My Reason for Writing Salon Talk

I just would like to say that I am absolutely honored and thankful to everyone who has taken the time to read and enjoy this novel. *Salon Talk – Topic of Discussion* is a fiction novel that elaborates on the drama filled life of my main character Rachelle aka Cognac. Her attraction to fast money making bad boys is detrimental to her but her thirst for cash and lust for the fast life keeps her living on the edge of danger. The breath taking events that transpire in her life are harsh enough to make a good girl turn wicked. *Salon Talk – Topic of Discussion* also highlights many of the spicy conversations and latest gossip that take place in the salons elaborating on love, relationships, cheating, jealousy, hating, sex, and drama. *Salon Talk – Topic of Discussion* addresses the many issues and pet peeves that you dread the most everyday and wish to be brought to the light. *It is definitely a page turner.*

Salon Talk – Topic of Discussion
FYI

The *Salon Talk* series of novels started off as a book of poems written in 2008 titled Salon Talk. The poems spoke on the numerous aspects of relationships. I took the most relative elements of your everyday experiences with love, pain, sex, cheating, spirituality, jealousy etc and poetically conjoined them. The silent cries and expressions that you have bottled up inside that seem to go unrecognized and unheard are addressed in this book. However this book sparked the idea of creating Salon Talk the novel.

Salon Talk the book of poems is scheduled as a duel release with *Salon Talk 2 – 187 Degrees of Danger* coming this summer.

As of now please enjoy as you read
Salon Talk – Topic of Discussion

True Beauty

True Beauty
Is not
Just your
Outer attractiveness
That meets ones eye
But is also
The reflection of the
Inner you

Your style
Your intelligence
Your loving personality
Accentuates
Your outer shell
Rendering that
Which is irresistible
Gorgeous

Make Up
Is a beautiful art
That we adore
But never feel
Ashamed

Of your natural beauty
For some feel
They have to hide
Behind multiple shades of
Lips stick and mascara
In order to feel appealing in public

You are a Goddess
You are astounding
You are Simply Beautiful

1

Three Days Before Christmas

12:47pm Cognac was on her way back from the mall, shopping for her man, Marcello for Christmas. She originally went into work this morning and remembered once she had gotten there that she had no clients scheduled. She figured that this would be the perfect day to shop for her man and take his gifts in the house and wrap them without him knowing. Marcello told her the night before that he had to get out and handle some serious business in the streets in the morning and he would practically be gone till late afternoon. She had a Macy's bag full of stuff she'd bought for him on her back seat; three designer outfits, and a large bottle of cologne. While driving up Greenfield road on her way home she noticed a Foot Locker shoe store and decided she wanted to get her boo some shoes. So she pulled into the parking lot, parked her car and got out. She set the alarm with her remote lock and walked inside. She caught the attention of everybody as she walked over to the Timberland boots displayed on the shelf. Cognac was ridiculous fine standing five foot seven in her black leather knee high boots with three inch heels. Her black Baby Phat jeans gripped her legs and juicy heart shaped ass perfectly. Her white waist length leather coat with the fur around the hood was nice looking on her. It had sleek black streak designs all through it looking sexy as hell. Her feather-wrap hair-doo was whipped to perfection; she knew she was the hottest thing breathing in the middle of winter.

"Can I help you with something today, beautiful?" The tall lanky sales-rep asked as he approached her.

"Yes, I need to get two pairs of Timberland boots, one in black, and the other in wheat. Both size eleven, please?" Cognac asked politely.

"Oh okay, I'll be right back with it, I mean with them, just give me a sec." The spellbound sales-rep said as he made his way back to the supply room.

Cognac stood there looking at all the ugly spaced out looking shoes they had on display. A guy walked up clean cut and fresh to def and glanced at her as he grabbed a pair of shoes off of the display and looked at them.

"You think these shoes look nice?" The tall six foot bald headed brotha with a well trimmed goatee asked.

"Naw, I don't like em." Cognac replied as she briefly looked at them and continued observing.

She noticed that he was nice looking, dressed nice, and smelled good, but wasn't fazed.

"So is Cognac your nickname, or is that your man's name?" He asked as he put the shoe back on the shelf and looked at her.

She glanced at him with a how the hell you know my name type of look on her face. She couldn't figure out where she might of knew him from so she asked "How do you know my name?"

"It's tattooed real sexy on your neck, Ms Lady. Don't worry, I ain't stalking you." Keith replied with a slight smile.

"Yeah, that's my name."

"Sounds interesting. So why they call you that?" Keith asked.

"Well, they call me Cognac because when I say what I got to say, I give it to you straight up like it is, with no ice, and no chaser." She answered, glancing at him then back at the shoes on display.

"I like that. I like a woman who can be straight up, and keep it real with me."

"I can't be no other way, but that."

"Damn, your realness makes you that much sexier, Ma." Keith replied.

"Thank you." Cognac replied, not giving him any eye contact.

"My bad sexy, my name's Keith. What's your real name or do you prefer to be called, Cognac?" Keith asked, extending his hand for a hand shake.

"It's Rachelle but I prefer, Cognac." She replied as she shook his hand.

"Well look Rachelle, I mean Cognac if you ain't doing nothing tonight why don't you let me take you out to dinner and show you a good time?"

"I'm sorry Keith I can't do that, I have a man."

"Damn, that nigga very lucky. I need a ride or die woman like you in my life."

"Well, it's some out there, you'll find one." Cognac replied as she continued browsing.

"Look, why don't you take my card just in case you decide you need a sponsor or something when that nigga start slippin." Keith said as he reached in his wallet and presented her with his business card.

"No thanks, my man is all the sponsor I need. Have a nice day, Keith." Cognac replied.

"Aight sexy have a good day then." Keith said as he turned and walked away.

The sales-rep returned with two boxes of Timberland boots in hands.

"Okay sweetie, here are your Timberland's." The sales rep said as he opened the boxes and showed her the merchandise.

"Thank you very much. Oh um can I get a pair of all white low top Air Force 1's in and eleven also?" Cognac asked as she took the two pairs of boots from him.

"No problem, I'll be right back. Matter of fact I'll just take them up to the counter and you can get them there." The sales-rep answered as he walked to the supply room.

"Thank you very much." Cognac replied.

Cognac looked in her purse and grabbed her cell phone to call and check on her son, Eric who was spending time with his father. She started dialing, and decided that she would just wait until she left the store to call. She then came across a picture of her man, Marcello and smiled. Briefly she reminisced of the various times that Marcello would surprise her by doing something very sweet to make her heart melt with love. Each time it would be something especially different yet simple such as a nice hot candle lit bubble bath right after a long hard day at work, or like the time when he had flowers delivered to her job just because. She regained her focus and placed the picture back in her purse. All while Cognac was shopping the saleslady at the register was lustfully eyeballing her the whole time. As Cognac made her way up front to pay for her shoes she sort of peeped ole girl checking her out.

"Hey, how are you doing?" Cognac asked politely as she placed the Timberlands up on the counter.

"I'm fine sweetie, how you doing today?" The cashier replied as she began ringing up the boots.

"I'm okay."

Cognac noticed the cashier had started playing with her tongue ring slowly flicking it in and out of her mouth and catching it with her teeth, as she was ringing her up.

"Are these your A1's?" The cashier asked.

"Yes they are."

"I see ole boy was trying to get at you."

"Yeah, that dudes something else; he just trying to get some ass that's all." Cognac said as she handed the cashier her charge card.

"I see why. You a sexy ass lady, hell I wouldn't mind tasting that myself." The cashier boldly stated as she handed her the copy of the receipt so she could sign it. For a split second Cognac was caught off guard and glanced at her but it wasn't something she hadn't heard before from a woman.

"Well, I don't do women sweetie, strictly men. Can't do the strap on thing." Cognac replied.

"Don't knock it till you've tried it."

"Have a nice day." Cognac said as she grabbed her bags and headed out the store.

"Oh, excuse me, miss you're leaving a bag here." The cashier spoke out.

Cognac turned and looked back, pointing to herself "You talking to me?"

"Yes, this bag right here is yours." The cashier said, holding the bag up. "I didn't buy this." Cognac replied as she stepped to the counter.

"I know, I was told to give this to you."

Cognac knew right then who it was from, and although she had all intensions of rejecting whatever it was she was curious about what was inside. She knew it was some shoes from the imprint in the bag and opened up the box very blasé. How lame and desperate she thought to herself of his actions as she looked at the pair of Air Force 1's. She started to close the box and hand it back to the cashier but noticed something in the mouth of the shoe. She peered closer and realized that it was a thick role of money. For a split second she paused in shock, but kept her composer, and closed the lid.

"Alright, have a good one." Cognac said as she took the bag along with her other bags and headed out the door. Vigilantly she observed her surroundings as she remotely unlocked her car door. Quickly she got in and tossed her bags in the passenger seat. She started her car, pulled out of the lot and drove off. She turned down a peaceful looking residential street, and eased in front of a foreclosed home in the middle of the block, and parked. She grabbed the money out of the shoe, and counted it down in between her legs so no one could see. She leafed through the stack of twenties, and fifties and counted five-hundred dollars which unfolded his business card at the end. Instinctively Cognac was going to just stick the money in her purse, throw Keith's card out of the window, and say she got the shoes herself, but she really loved Marcello, and wanted to be completely open and honest with him about everything. She figured he'd respect her more if she told him exactly what went down so she put everything like it was and drove home. After ten minutes of driving she arrived at her street and made a left. As she approached the house she was surprised to see Marcello's car in the driveway. She thought that he would be gone but she was actually happy that he was there. She turned her car off, grabbed her bags and walked up to the door. If Marcello was to ask her what was in the bags she would simply tell him don't worry about what's in the bags but worry about how she was about to give him the business after she put the bags down and take her clothes off. She put the key in the knob and opened the door. "Baby" she called out to Marcello as she stepped inside. Once again to her surprise Marcello always seems to know the perfect way to catch her off guard by doing something unexpected. She took a deep breath, closed her eyes, and shook her head with a smile as she found a gorgeous assortment of flowers wrapped up and strapped with a beautiful ribbon on the counter. She walked into the den just to her right and sat her shopping bags down then took off her coat and hung it in the guest closet. She turned around and grabbed a brown paper bag from out of one of the shopping bags and walked back into the kitchen. She pulled out a bottle of chilled red wine and sat it down on the kitchen table. She grabbed two wine glasses from out of the cabinet just above the counter and sat them next to the wine. She turned around and joyfully picked the flowers up, put them to her nose then pleasantly sniffed. All she could think is how her man has no idea how she's about to wear his ass out in the nastiest way. She sat the flowers back down on the counter top. She eased up the hallway to see if he was in the livingroom sleeping on the couch but he wasn't. She figured maybe he was upstairs knocked out and if he was she was about to give him the best oral awakening ever imagined. She heard the faint sound of slow jams playing from her stereo in her room upstairs. She calmly eased up the stairs swaying her hips from left to right and was slightly alarmed by what she thought was voices that were not coming from the radio. With an I KNOW MUTHAFUCKIN WELL IT BETTER NOT BE type of look on her face as she walked up the stairs. Her blood percolated and her heart felt like it was pounding its way through the middle of her chest. Hell has no explanation for the hate that was flowing through her veins, engulfing her soul after hearing a female's voice utter very low and sneaky "You think that's her?" Once she made it to the top of the stair case and entered her room she saw Marcello and her friend, Tamara rushing to put their clothes on. There was a metal folding chair leaning up against the wall and she immediately grabbed it. Marcello's eyes lit up like Volks Wagon headlights as he noticed Cognac running at them!

"Hold on baby! Wait a minute!" Marcello yelled out as he put his arm up to protect himself.

"Fuck holding on, bitch!" Cognac retorted as she violently swung the chair and cracked him in the arm and head, making him fall back up against the wall.

Tamara rolled off the left side of the bed trying to get the fuck out of the way. Cognac then swung the chair riotously at Tamara as she barely ducked out of the way making Cognac smash the radio. Cognac swung the chair back at her again and missed, mistakenly smashing the portrait on the wall after the chair slipped out of her hands. Marcello had quickly grabbed Cognac from behind trying to contain her making her drop the chair.

"GET YO SHIT AND GET THE FUCK OUT OF HERE!!!" Marcello yelled at Tamara while trying to avoid Cognac's sharp heals as she stomped at his feet.

"Nigga, let me the fuck go! I'm bout to kill this bitch." Cognac screamed as she wildly tried shaking loose.

"Bitch you ain't gone do shit to me!" Tamara replied as she put on her pants and shirt.

"OH BITCH YOU RUNNING YO FUCKIN MOUTH?!!! Nigga, I said let me the fuck go!" Cognac yelled as she finally managed to turn around and scratch Marcello's face.

"Get yo ass the fuck on!" Marcello yelled at Tamara again.

"Oh you trying to protect that bitch?!" Cognac yelled furiously as she bit him on the neck.

Marcello yelled in pain as Cognac broke free and ran after Tamara. He knew that if Cognac caught up to Tamara she probably would unconsciously kill that girl. He immediately ran behind her trying to catch her. Tamara was about to put on her coat while heading for the door. Out of the corner of her eye she noticed Cognac running towards her reckless as an avalanche and threw a punch but couldn't connect because Marcello grabbed her once again.

"Nigga, stop fucking grabbing me!" Cognac shouted as she fiercely tried punching him in the nuts and stomping his feet to get away.

Tamara turned around with a mean scowl on her face, feeling no remorse for fucking Cognac's man.

"Bitch, don't keep running up on me!" Tamara stressed.

"Bitch, you going to disrespect me up in my house, in my bed with my man and you going to run yo fuckin mouth?! Marcello, let me the fuck go." Cognac said eloquently as she tried breaking loose from Marcello's strong grip.

"Tamara, get yo dumb ass the fuck out of here!" Marcello yelled.

"Dumb ass?! You wasn't just saying that shit earlier! It was more like damn she don't slob and choke on this dick like you do. Remember?" Tamara spitefully said as she stood there scoffing at both of them.

Marcello got tired of trying to keep them apart and just let Cognac go and stepped back leaving nothing between them but air and opportunity.

"Okay, fuck it." Marcello said as he looked at Tamara like he felt sorry for her stupid ass.

"Now what was you saying, bitch?" Cognac sinisterly asked as she walked up on her.

Tamara threw a jab but Cognac was on point and ducked then came up with a stern left upper cut catching Tamara right on the chin causing her mouth to bleed. Tamara threw another punch and missed as Cognac caught her square in the nose with a fierce right cross. Tamara was dizzy and intimidated and wanted no parts of Cognac. Tamara glanced at Marcello like you ain't gonna grab this bitch and then tried to run. Cognac reached and clutched a hand full of Tamara's hair and slung her head right onto the corner of the kitchen counter, and then rammed her head against the wall behind her. Then she spun her around and hurled her head through the glass of the kitchen table making her cut her hands on sharp splinter fragments once she hit the floor. The bottle of wine and wine glasses collapsed and shattered leaving wine splattered everywhere. Cognac charged at her but slipped and fell backwards onto the floor after the heel of her boot snapped. Tamara quickly got up, grabbed her purse off the floor and ran out the door with no shoes or socks on her feet. Swiftly she ran across the hard frozen concrete and asphalt to her aunt's car that she parked across the street. She franticly pulled her keys from her purse and unlocked the door. She got inside and slammed the door shut, immediately locking the door behind her. Cognac ran up on the car rapidly pulling on the door handle trying to open it. Angrily she kicked the driver's side window and then the side view mirror shattering it. Tamara nervously put her keys in the ignition then started the car and sped off. Exhaustedly Cognac walked back into the house with a look of spurning disbelief written on her face. She walked over by the kitchen sink and leaned back up against the counter. Marcello had gotten dressed and walked back down stairs. He proceeded into the kitchen and noticed her standing there with a facial expression that was hollow and unpredictable. The vibe in the room was cold as a December grave. He took a few more steps towards her then stopped because he felt that if he got any closer things could get very violent. Marcello pretty much knew that there was nothing he could say to make things better. He was hesitant to speak but mustered up the nerve to do so. With a pathetic, shameful look on his face he uttered "Baby...I'm sorry. I wasn't thinking." Marcello took another step closer and stopped as she open the silverware drawer. She reached inside and pulled out a butcher knife then looked back towards him, ominously staring at his chest. A tear trickled down her peeved face with her lips and jaws tightened. "Baby, I, I can explain." Marcello pathetically uttered. The sound of his voice roused her hate the more he spoke. She reached inside the drawer again and pulled out a second butcher knife. She was no killer...but dangerous love affairs will introduce the most innocent people to a crime of passion. Marcello was momentarily petrified for he had never seen this erratic side of Coney before. He quickly came to his senses and left out of the house.

2

Cognac and Conversation

9:00pm **Lacey's Bar & Grill** had a nice crowd. Everyone was hyped and rooting as they watched the **Pistons** beat up on the **Celtics** on the TV's mounted all around the bar.

Regina, Benita and Cynthia sat at their table staring at Cognac with their mouths open as they engaged in serious conversation.

"So you mean to tell me that this fool brought your friend who was at the party up in your house, and screwed her?!" Benita asked as she looked at her in disbelief.

"Hell yeah, I couldn't believe that shit." Cognac replied as she sipped her Hennessey and shook her head.

"Mannnnn, oh my God! I wish I was there, I would've beat that bitch's ass." Cynthia added.

"That's what I was doing. Her ass lucky I snapped the heel on my new damn boot, I promise you she wouldn't have got away."

"And I knew that night when we was at the party, that bitch was jealous of you. Just by the way she kept looking at you when you weren't looking. And just how she was too friendly with your man; constantly walking pass him trying to be seen. Bitches ain't shit sometimes." Cynthia said.

"I don't know why woman be desperate like that. I wouldn't make myself look like a low down little hoe trying to mess with another woman's man, especially my supposed to be home girl's man. Please, it's too many dudes out here to be playing them little juvenile girl games." Regina added.

"Niggas ain't shit, bottom line!" Cynthia said as she sipped her drink.

"Hold up, you gotta be fair, you can't say that about all men, just like men can't say that about all women. It's some good brotha's out there; you just have to be selective about who you allow in your life." Regina said.

"They all pretend to be good brotha's but soon as they get in good and comfortable, they mess up." Cognac replied.

"I bet you that guy Devin that you brought over to the house one time was Mr. Right. His character, the things he was into was just right. This Marcello guy, I knew something was up with him. He was loud, and flamboyant, a drug dealer, and seemed to have nothing humble and positive about himself." Regina added.

"Whatever happened to that Devin guy anyway?" Benita asked.

"I don't know I just wasn't feeling him. I mean, he just was too nice." Cognac answered.

"To nice, are you serious?" Regina asked as she leaned forward.

"...yeah, I don't want a guy that I feel like I can just dog out." Cognac replied.

"I can't stand no weak man. That just irritates the hell out of me." Cynthia added.

"Why does a man have to be considered weak just because he's nice to you? If you don't want to dog a brotha out, then control your emotions and actions and just don't dog him out then." Regina said.

Men-Tal

"I'm sorry I want my man to have a little thug thizzle about him." Cognac impressed.

"I feel you on that, girl." Cynthia concurred as she high fived her.

"Well, I don't mean to bust your bubble, but it was that thug thizzle that got you in the middle of this bull shizzle my nizzle." Benita added as she pointed at Cognac.

"Hey, I'm with Cynthia, fuck niggas." Cognac replied as she sipped her drink.

Benita's cell phone rang, and she answered it.

"Hello?............Yeah we in here..........When Y'all come in just look to your right, and you'll see us sitting down." Benita said and hung up the phone.

"Girl, who you got coming up here?" Regina asked.

"My boy Jonnie, and a few of his boys." Benita answered.

"This was supposed to be girl's night out." Cynthia stated.

"And these are things that happened during girl's night out." Benita said as she looked towards the entrance.

"They better not be ugly, I know that much." Cognac said.

They all laughed in agreement.

"I know we still going out to Club Exclusive after we eat and leave here, right?" Peaches asked with an eyebrow raised.

"Hell yeah, we done got all dressed up and sexy too. We there, boo." Cognac replied.

"Well when these dudes get here I hope they ain't trying to go over to the club with us! Because um, I ain't trying to take sand and water to the beach...unless they fine as hell. You know what I'm saying!" Peaches said humorously nudging Cognac on the arm.

"That must be them right there. Yup, because there go Jonnie in that Detroit cap." Benita said.

"Are you serious?" Peaches replied with a slight oh hell nall expression on her face and eyes bucked.

Jonnie and his boys stood there for a second looking around, two slim dudes and two heavy set dudes. Benita waved her hand in the air so they could see them.

"Oh hell nall. Are you kidding me? How you gone be fat as hell, and look like a stressed out Sammy Davis Jr.?" Cognac uttered to her girls as the dudes were walking up.

Men-Tal

"The other fat guy got on a tight ass muscle man move something shirt, but that gut looks like he's been curling Junior Whoppers to his mouth instead of curling dumb bells. That's gone be Regina's future baby daddy." Benita said.

"You crazier than six muthafucka's! Oops see you got me cussin, but you smoking if you think that's me right there." Regina replied.

Benita got up and hugged Jonnie as he and his boys approached the table.

"Everybody, this is my friend Jonnie. Jonnie, this is Regina, Cognac, and Cynthia." Benita said introducing him to her friends.

"Hey, how are Y'all doing? Well, this is my boy Damon, Big Tone, and Big Jay." Jonnie said as he introduced his boys as well.

They decided that they would connect another table to the table the ladies were sitting at and then they pulled up some chairs next to the ladies and sat down with them.

After seven or eight minutes of cool conversation Cognac heard her cell phone ringing and then reached in the pocket of her waist length fur coat hanging on the back of her chair and grabbed it. She looked at the caller I.D. then closed her eyes and sighed to herself in slight disgust. She excused herself from the table to go into the restroom so she could have a little privacy and answer her phone. As she got up people's eyes were transfixed on her stunning outfit, a Fox fur halter top that revealed her caramel flat stomach, and cream spandex pants that road her hips and curves dangerously. She started walking and immediately became the Topic of Discussion of many people's conversation at the bar. It was like a sexual paralysis for some who could do nothing but swallow their saliva, fantasize it's her that they tasted, and utter that one common word...DAYUM. "Why do you keep calling my phone?! What do you want?...... Don't worry about where the hell I'm at! Go find Tamara." Cognac stressed and hung up. She sat her purse down on the sink, placed her phone inside and pulled out a comb and started fiddling with her hair. She didn't think that she was being looked at the whole time she'd walked in by someone peering through the gap in the stall just behind her. The toilet flushed and then the stall door opened. An attractive lady walked out and approached the sink, turned on the water and started washing her hands. A couple of times the lady glanced over at Cognac, but Cognac never looked her way, she just kept feathering her hair. The lady glanced at her a couple of more times and Cognac asked "Is there any particular reason you keep looking over here at me?" Cognac continued doing her hair. The lady remained silent for about seven seconds and replied "I was just checking out my competition. Normally all eyes are on me because I'm the finest thing in the building but I must admit you're a fine ass woman. I see why my date kept looking over at you when you were sitting at the table." "Well, I'm not trying to compete with you nor do I want your man, I have enough things on my plate right now. Have a good one." Cognac replied as she grabbed her purse and walked out. The lady just enviously stared at Cognac's ass through the mirror until the bathroom door shut behind her. Cognac walked back to the table and sat down. By that time the waitress had come over and took more orders. They were having a hell of a conversation and Jonnie brought Cognac in on it.

"Hey, Cognac I gotta question for you. I just need to get another point of view on this hot topic." Jonnie expressed.

"Go for it, I'm all ears." Cognac replied.

"Alright, why is it that women feel the need to keep their age a secret when they meet a man, but they want a man to be up front and honest with them from the jump?" Jonnie asked.

"What? We ain't suppose to tell y'all our ages, that's Lady Law." Cognac answered with a smile.

"That's right, boo. Lady Law!" Benita concurred.

"Now hold on Sheriff there's a flaw in y'all's Lady Law called double standard. Y'all want to withhold, and keep your age a secret but if a man withholds the fact that he has a woman when he meets you and decides to tell you when he gets ready, preferably after he gets the cookies, y'all would say he was wrong and you wouldn't talk to no more." Jonnie stressed.

"Aw hell nall, you can't use that because that ain't the same. You gotta come with something better than that my brotha." Regina replied.

"Us women have a curtain mystique about us. If we keep you inquisitive then perhaps you'll keep seeking and sincerely get to know us and age won't matter. And by that time we will know if we should gamble with one chip or put it all out there on the table." Cynthia added.

"Well, inquiring minds want to know. How old are you?" Damon asked with a smooth, suave look on his face looking at Cynthia.

"Nice try, but it ain't that easy, sir." Cynthia replied with a smirk on her face.

"Yeah, okay. I see you like to play them chase games, dog chase the cat." Damon replied.

The conversation had gotten good and spicy, but everyone sort of quieted down and listened when Jonnie's boy, Nate who had been sort of quiet the whole time decided he wanted to add his point of view.

"Y'all mind if I add my two cents?" Nate asked.

"Go ahead, this is an open conversation. We ain't gone chop you up yet." Benita said jokingly.

"First let me say that age is like wine, it only gets better with time. Way back in the day women were looked upon as old maids if they weren't married by the age of eighteen, nineteen, or twenty. And even though we've evolved in time many women still unconsciously apply that old concept to themselves therefore sparking insecurity when it comes to their age." Nate expressed.

"So you saying our perception of age is out dated?" Cognac asked.

"Exactly, age doesn't matter like people say it does. Actually it's more about looks before age." Nate said.

"What? Looks before age?" Benita asked with an incredulous look on her face.

"Yes, looks before age. For example, I'll date a fifty-five year old woman who looks twenty-five before I date a twenty-five year old woman who looks fifty-five." Nate stressed.

"Yes sir." Jonnie seriously concurred.

"Hey, that's how Stella got her groove back." Cynthia replied.

"Oh my God." Cognac said as she covered her eyes with her hand.

"What? What's wrong?" Regina asked.

"Oh, hell nall! What the hell is he doing here?" Cynthia asked as she looked at the entrance.

Marcello walked through the front door looking for Cognac. He looked around and noticed her sitting down with everybody. He took a deep breath and walked over to the table. Cognac immediately got pissed, but decided she wasn't about to clown on him. Regina, Benita, and Cynthia got up and stood in his way so that he didn't cause no drama. Marcello stopped and looked at them nonchalantly, and then looked passed them trying to talk to Cognac.

"Coney, can I talk to you for a minute?" Marcello asked.

"Marcello, why don't you leave? This is not a good time to talk to her right now." Regina suggested.

"I ain't trying to start no problems with Y'all, I need to talk to my woman."

"That ain't your woman, you disrespectful nigga! Go get that braud you was fuckin in her house!" Cynthia said emphatically.

"Ain't nobody even talking to you, stupid hoe!" Marcello retorted repulsively.

"Who the fuck you calling a hoe, bitch?!" Cynthia responded furiously.

"I got your bitch! You better shut the fuck up!" Marcello stressed, pointing his finger in her face.

The manager noticed what was going on, and immediately picked up the phone and called the police. The security noticed as well and made their way over to stop the violence from happening. One of the dudes that were sitting at the table got up and tried to address the problem.

"Yo my man, why don't you go the hell on, dog?" Big Tone stressed, grimacing at him.

"Nigga, shut the fuck up! The only reason you got heart to say something to me is because your boys is around, you fat bitch!" Marcello impressed as he grimmed him.

Jonnie and his boys were ready to handle Marcello if they had to but Marcello didn't give a fuck.

"Dog, get the fuck on with that bullshit, playboy." Jonnie said emphatically.

"Nigga fuck you, and fuck yo muthafuckin boys to, bitch ass nigga!" Marcello yelled at Jonnie as he started walking up on them.

Security walked up between them and separated them. They escorted Marcello out of the bar immediately. Marcello yanked his arm away from security, and grimed them as he walked out. Police whipped up on the scene as Marcello was headed to his car, and got out on him. They placed handcuffs on him, and put him in the back of the car, and ran his I.D. They saw that he had warrants for traffic violations and took him to the precinct.

After about thirty minutes or so they all decided that it was about time to call it a night. The ladies definitely decided they weren't going to the club after all the drama jumped off. A serious buzz, unnecessary B.S, and just a few hours of sleep is a recipe for a pounding headache in the morning just before work.

Essence of Beauty and Soul

3

A Beautiful Day At Essential Beauty Salon

It was a surprising yet extraordinary day at Essential Beauty Salon. EBS had gained a reputation over the course of a couple of years for doing astounding hairstyles for women and had generated a very nice clientele. The owners Mrs. Sarah Langston and Bob Langston both in their sixties were getting ready to make a very surprising announcement. Bob, just behind Sarah stood in the center isle with her lovely smile, and gained every ones attention.

"Good Afternoon everyone, it is such a beautiful day and a pleasure to be surrounded by such beautiful people. It always makes my day to come in here and witness so much creativity and talent. I love to see all the various hair-styles and women walking out of here looking like they belong on the cover of a magazine. I love all of the thought provoking, and healthy conversations that go on throughout the day. I have learned so much from you all. This is my husband and I's twenty-seventh marriage anniversary." Mrs. Langston declared just as everyone started clapping.

"I also would like to say that today is the second year anniversary of Essential Beauty Salon. (Everyone clapped) And I am honored to be a part of such a remarkable establishment and staff members. However, I just want to say this and get it on out of the way. I am partaking in a new venture in my life, I have my own radio talk show on channel 98.9 fm every night from 8pm to 10pm. (Everyone applauded) We have come to an agreement that Regina will assume the managerial position based on her credentials and hopefully one day soon take on the ownership as well. (Everyone applauded) Well that's all I have to say for now, I will miss you all, thank you and have a blessed day." Mrs. Langston said as tears dripped down her face.

Mr. Langston hugged his wife and thanked everyone as well. Regina, with eyes watered walked over and hugged Mrs. Langston as the three of them walked out of the front door.

After about forty-five minutes had gone past and the emotions calmed it was back to business as usual. Gifted hands, and accurate vision helped devise some of the most astonishing hair-doo's. Afro's, quick weaves, presses, lace-front wigs etcetera were donned by some of Detroit finest women. And of course in every salon there's always the *Topic of Discussion*.

"Why is that when a man meets a woman for the first time, he's loving how sexy she looks, but when she becomes his woman her sexy style becomes a problem?" Benita proposed a question to anyone who wanted to reply.

Benita's client sighed out loud, and then expressed herself.

"Because the man is stupid and insecure. He don't want no other man trying to holla at his woman, and if that's the case then get with a ugly chic, flat out." Lynette said as

Benita braided her hair, preparing it for a sew-in.

"Why is it that he's gotta be insecure? Why can't it be that a man just wants his woman to look presentable when she steps out, and represent him in a good way?" Duce asked as he gave his client a pedicure.

"Well if he saw how she dressed when he first got with her then why all of a sudden get an attitude and change the game up down the line?" Lynette asked, sneering at him.

"Because when he first meets her he's attracted to the provocative look, even if it's a little bit extra provocative as long as she ain't looking sleazy and trampy. He also respects the fact that if she's single she can dress however she wants to dress but once he gets deeper into the relationship and feelings get involved he wants his woman to look and be presentable and respectable." Duce stated.

"I guess it all depends on what your definition of presentable and respectable is." Lynette replied.

"Well, to each is own. I know I wouldn't want my woman out here looking like a thirsty hoe or an attention whore." Duce said as he glanced at her for a second and continued his pedicure.

"Why she gotta be an attention whore because she wants to dress sexy?" Benita asked.

"Come on now, you know that when you get ready to leave the house, and you put on your make up, and check and make sure your ass is looking right in your jeans that you want to look good for whoever is around you." Duce answered.

"Why she just can't want to look good for herself?" Lynette asked.

"That's bull; you can't convince me that y'all don't do it for the attention. Everything y'all do from putting on make up to barely sliding in skin tight clothes is for the attention from somebody else." Duce emphasized.

"You act like y'all men don't like attention just like women do." Lynette impressed.

"I ain't saying that we don't like attention, but it ain't like how y'all women need attention. Y'all gotta be told all day everyday that Y'all look good or Y'all gone have a problem." Duce replied.

"LOOK, Bottom line is if a woman likes to dress sexy or revealing that's her prerogative and if a man don't like it then he shouldn't try to get to know her in the first place. That's what y'all get for thinking with your small head. Me personally, I think all this looks stuff is over rated, and trouble waiting to happen. Just give me a dude that's just ridiculous ugly, and I'll be straight." Benita added as she continued braiding.

"Hold on, boo. I was agreeing with you all the way up to that last statement.

"He'll treat you like the best thing on this planet."

"You're only gone be with him for the money." Lynette stated with an eyebrow raised.

"That ain't true." Benita replied.

"So, you mean to tell me that you can be honestly be faithful to a guy who you are not attracted to?" Lynette asked.

"Yes I can."

"I couldn't do that. I got to be able to enjoy looking at whoever I'm with." Lynette said.

"Hey, that will be your loss." Benita replied.

"Okay since it ain't about the money. What if he's ugly and broke?" Lynette asked.

"Girl I almost curled a lock of hair out of yo head, talking that crazy mess." Benita said as she leaned forward, looking down at Lynette.

"Hey, you're the one who said it ain't about the money." Lynette replied.

"Hey, I can't be messing around with them undesirable looking Mo-Fro's unless they got some serious cash. I mean just ridiculous ugly with a Siberian Donkey face. And don't let em be ugly and a big back to, Oh Hell Nall I can't do that." Duce stressed.

"What's a big back?" Lynette asked.

"Somebody that's just two tons of fun, big, somebody with a real wide back or what people like to say, heavy set." Duce answered.

Peaches client, Rhonda was heavy set and terribly offended by Duce's remarks about heavy-set people.

"Your words are very offensive, sir." Rhonda said as she slightly frowned at Duce.

Duce had forgotten that she was even in the salon, and looked back and replied "My bad." He snickered as he turned around.

"Yeah, you laughing but at least I ain't over there looking like a dirty looking skinny ass Meer cat either." Rhonda said causing a slight roar of snickers.

"Oh you got jokes huh? Well at least I ain't over there looking like Buffy the Big Mac slayer either." Duce replied causing some to bust out laughing.

"And you so skinny, your heart beat looks like a damn bird trying to break out a cage." Rhonda replied.

"Yeah, and you so fat and greedy you can smell the seasoning on frozen food."

"Well you look like you need to eat you some food because your collar bone looks like a damn curtain rod going across your damn chess."

"Alright, calm down Y'all, this is still a professional hair salon not a comedy club." Regina said as she walked back in the door trying not to laugh at their jokes.

Regina noticed Cognac was not at her station. Cognac had been quiet all day, not really saying a word. Regina walked to the back room and opened the door and went in. She saw Cognac sort of curled up in a chair, holding her stomach, and walked over to her.

"Cognac, what's the matter?"

"I don't know. I'm having some serious cramps going on."

"Did you eat something that wasn't right?"

"Nall, nothing out of the ordinary."

"How long you been feeling this way?" Regina asked as she pulled another chair up close to Cognac.

"I started feeling a slight sharp pain in my stomach like a couple of days ago. Then today I really started feeling it." Cognac answered, frowning as she curled a little tighter after feeling another sharp pain.

"Maybe you need to go get that checked out. You think you're pregnant?"

"Girl, don't even put nothing like that into the atmosphere. I hope to God I ain't pregnant."

"Well why don't you let me take you to the hospital and let the doctor check you out."

"Ima just call my Doctor and try to set an appointment with him for tomorrow."

"You think you'll be alright waiting until tomorrow?"

"Yeah, I should be good. If not maybe you can take me to emergency if it starts getting worse."

"That's already a done deal. Why don't you go home and get you some rest?"

"Yeah, that's what Ima do."

Regina sat there lightly rubbing her arm trying to comfort her.

"I love you, cuz." Regina said.

"I love you to, big cuz." Cognac replied as she managed to smile a little.

4

A Double Life

Cynthia drove eastward up the snowy, unplowed 6mile rd on her way home while talking to Damon on the phone. She and Damon had been secretly kickin it pretty good on the phone ever since Jonnie and his boys came up to the bar yesterday.

"I cannot believe I just fucked you, and I just met you yesterday." Cynthia said, shaking her head.

"Did you like it?" Damon asked.

"Yeah, it was cool, not bad."

"I'm ready for round two later on tonight if you can get back out."

"See, you trying to get me in trouble."

"No I ain't, I just want you to put all that ass on me again, damn that shit felt so fuckin good."

"Oh did it?"

"Hell yeah it did."

"I like that curve action you got going on there."

"Oh really, Did you like the way it tasted?"

"Mmmmmmmm yes, I can still taste you in my mouth right now. I can still feel the head jabbing the back of my throat."

"Damn baby, I love how you say shit like that."

"Did you like tasting me?"

"Hell fuck yeah, I did. I like how you rode my face with that juicy round ass of yours."

"Awww, did you? You want me to do it again?"

"Hell yeah I do, but you know what I want you to do for me right now?"

"What's that?" Cynthia asked as she looked at her phone to see who was calling her on the other line, and ignored it.

"I want you to take your middle finger, stick in your mouth and wet it."

Cynthia rotated her tongue around her finger as she stuck it in her mouth and passionately sucked on it as she slowly pulled it out.

"Okay, I did it."

"Now I want you to do everything I tell you to do and just imagine the things I'm saying to you."

"Okay, Daddy."

Cynthia was game and did everything he asked of her. She pulled up her dress, slid her thong to the side, and rotated her middle finger in a circular motion around her vaginal lips. She stuck the same middle finger back in her mouth and moaned as she stuck her hand beneath her dress and gently stroked her clit. Breathing heavily she momentarily closed her eyes and started fingering herself, building up to cum. She opened her eyes to look at the road real quick.

"Oh fuck! Shit, shit!" Cynthia shouted out as she slammed on the brakes, partially sliding through a red light into oncoming traffic.

"Damn baby I got you cumin like that?" Damon asked, giving himself undeserving credit.

"No nigga, you just made me slide through a damn red light, bout to get me killed." Cynthia retorted, putting her car in reverse and pulling back in front of the traffic light.

"Well you know they say women can't drive." Damon said, being sarcastic.

"Boy, don't make me come through this phone on you." Cynthia said as she pulled off after the light turned green.

"Actually I would love for your ass to cum through the phone just so I can taste you again."

"You a nasty ass freak." Cynthia lustfully emphasized.

"You know your ass like that shit."

"Damn, the police right behind me, Ima call you right back!" Cynthia said as she quickly hung up her phone.

The police put on the sirens signaling her to pull over, and she did. She peeped through the rearview to see how fast the officer was getting out of the car, and immediately unfastened the top three buttons to her dress she was wearing exposing the top portion of her breast. She placed her purse on the floor of the passenger seat, and positioned herself very sexy as the officer approached.

"License and registration, mam?" Officer Johnson asked as he stood in front of her trying not to stare at her breast to hard while he was talking to her.

Cynthia leaned over to grab her purse off of the floor and showed the officer what a nice round thoroughbred sista ass really looked like.

"Here you are, Officer Johnson. I can't find my registration." Cynthia said as she handed him her license.

"Cynthia, huh? You know you just broke a few laws, don't you?" Officer Johnson asked as he kept glancing at her breast.

"I know. I didn't mean to slide through that light, but I didn't see that ice patch." Cynthia said as she looked up at him with guilt-ridden eyes.

"That's because you were busy talking on your cell phone."

"I'm sorry, but it was a very important phone call, and I wasn't on there long."

"And you don't have your registration either." Officer Johnson emphasized as he entertained lustful thoughts.

"Are you going to give me a ticket?" Cynthia asked sympathetically.

"Unless you convince me not to." Officer Johnson said, rubbing his hands together, and licking his lips.

"Straight up? You gone flex your power like that huh?" Cynthia asked, starring at him from the waist up.

"Give me your phone."

"For what?"

"Give me your phone like I said before I write yo ass all these tickets." Officer Johnson impressed.

Cynthia shook her head and smirked as she handed him the phone. Officer Johnson took her phone and dialed his cell number so that he could have her number. He put the phone up to his ear.

"Hello, aye yo my man, don't be calling my woman phone no fuckin mo." Officer Jonson said as he backed up a couple of steps with her phone.

"Don't be calling nobody on my phone. Gimme my phone." Cynthia said as she got out of her car.

"Come get it."

Cynthia walked up to him and grabbed her phone then looked to see who he had called.

"You better not had called nobody." Cynthia said as she realized that he only called his phone.

"I just wanted you to get out of the car so that I could see what it looked like." Officer Johnson said as he delectably looked her up and down.

"Y'all police officers something else, always want to control somebody. Why you ain't just flex your power like you did a minute ago and have me get out the car instead of taking my phone?" Cynthia asked.

"Oh I'm saving that power for the next time I see your sexy ass."

"Alright I'll call you, I gotta go." Cynthia said as she got back in her car.

"Next time I see you, I'm strip searching you."

"I gotta man so don't be calling my phone like that."

"I ain't bout to mess your game up, just tell me when the best time to call you."

"In the mornings."

"Alright, be safe out here, sexy." Officer Johnson said as he started walking back to his car.

Cynthia honked the horn as she pulled off then picked up her cell phone and called Damon.

"Damn, what happened, he give you a ticket?" Damon asked after picking up the phone.

"Hell nall, the nigga just basically took my phone and called his phone so he'll have my number." Cynthia said as she made a right turn down her street, Warwick.

"Get the fuck outta here."

"I ain't playing with you. He pulled me over, and asked me for license and registration which he didn't give a damn about because he was too busy staring at my tits and thighs. Then he asked me for my phone and when I handed it to him he dialed his phone so he'll have my number."

"Damn, that nigga just police pimped yo ass. He supposed to be out protecting and serving the streets and this nigga trying to protect and serve it to you in the sheets."

"Its crime all out here in the streets and this fool too busy trying to get a nut off."

"Aye, just to switch the subject for a second. Why don't you make up a reason to get away later on so we can have round two?"

"See, you trying to get me in trouble."

"No I ain't, baby, I just wanna feel you some more. That shit was good."Damon impressed.

"I don't know, my man be on me."

"He ain't gone know. Tell him you going out with your girls or better yet tell him one of your girls had something drastic happen and you wanna be there for her."

As Cynthia drove up her street she noticed at the last second that her boyfriend, Cedric was parked in front of her house. Immediately her heartbeat rushed.

"Aye, I gotta call you back!" Cynthia uttered quickly as she hung up her phone.

She pulled into her driveway hoping Cedric didn't see her on the phone. She tried to gather herself as she put the car in park, quickly ran her fingers through her hair. She thought of numerous lies to explain why she was on the phone and didn't answer when he called if he asked. They got out of their cars simultaneously, shutting the doors behind them. Cedric was curious as of why she didn't answer her phone but wasn't about to start accusing her off the rip. Cynthia figured she'd play the I'm irritated, I don't want to be bothered card if Cedric started asking questions as she walked around the back of the car headed for the porch.

"Wsup babe?" Cedric asked as he walked up to the house.

"Nothing." Cynthia replied sort of dry as she stepped to the door and stuck her key in to unlock it.

"Where are you on your way from?" Cedric calmly asked as he stepped up on the porch.

Cynthia rolled her eyes upward and exhaled through her nose with her lips tightly shut then replied "My Moms house." She opened the door and stepped in. Cedric stepped in and shut the door behind him.

"What's wrong with you?" Cedric asked as he stepped up a couple of stairs to his right, into the kitchen.

"Nothing, I'm just irritated." Cynthia said with an incredulous look on her face.

"Well, don't take your irritations out on me, I ain't did shit to you. And besides, you weren't just too irritated when you just pulled up laughing and giggling on the phone. Who was you on the phone with?" Cedric asked with an eyebrow raised.

"I was on the phone with my girl. I can't talk to my girl now?"

"Well how come you can smile and laugh with your girl, and when it comes to me you all irritated?"

"Damon, I ain't about to argue with you right now." Cynthia impressed with a fierce attitude.

"Damon? Who the fuck is Damon?" Cedric asked with a twisted face.

"I didn't mean to say Damon."

"I can care less with what you meant. Who the hell is Damon?"

"Da, Damon is one of them um, um little kids that was over my Moms house getting on my nerves."

"You are so full of shit; you can't even get your words out without stuttering."

"Ain't nobody full of shit, Cedric. I'm just stressed right now, and I want to go lay down." Cynthia emphasized as she glanced at him.

"We were supposed to be doing something, you asked me to meet you here, and I did. You pulled up to the house talking and laughing, but once you saw me you all of a sudden stressed out, and need to lay down. Why is that?!" Cedric asked, furiously.

Cedric walked up on her feeling in his heart that she was lying. He saw that her clothes and hair-doo looked kind of scruffy when she never goes anywhere looking less than on point.

"Cedric, don't even start with me right now." Cynthia said as she shook her head.

"Why your clothes and hair all shabby looking?"

"What are you talking about? Please don't start; I just wanna rest my head."

"Who were you talking to on the phone, Cynthia?"

"I told you I was talking to my girl."

"Your girl who?"

"My girl, Tamika. Why you asking me all of these questions about who I'm on the phone with? I don't be all on you about who you be on the phone with."

"That's because you just pick up my phone and just go through it without saying nothing." Cedric said as he snatched her phone and looked to see the last person she was talking to.

"Give me my phone, Cedric!" Cynthia yelled as he dialed the last number.

Cynthia worriedly tried grabbing her phone, afraid of how Cedric was going to react when Damon picked and answered. Fortunately for her the call went to the voicemail which had not been set up yet. Cedric handed her back her phone, and Cynthia took it with a slight attitude.

"Cynthia let me tell you something. I done gave you my all and shared with you my last. You better not be playing me, and that's all I got to say." Cedric said with a scowled look on his face as he turned and walked out the door.

5

One Thing After Another

3:37pm **Duce had just got** off work from up at the Salon and was driving eastward up 8mile rd headed home to his apartment. The city had sent their trucks out to lay salt down on the ground, but it was still wet and somewhat slippery. Duce was giggin and jammin to the music as he weaved through traffic recklessly. His cell phone rang so he grabbed it off of his side holster and answered it.

"Hello?" Duce answered with eyebrows crinkled inward.

"Yes, can I speak to Kevin Felton please?"

"Speaking. Who is this?"

"This is Ms. Latamara Carter calling on behalf of Hilton Green Apartment Collection Department."

"Oh…….okay um, I can send the money in two weeks if that's okay. My job messed on my hours and—" Duce said as he was cut off.

"Sir, I am so sorry but it's not in my hands to make that decision. We have already made arrangements with you on your delinquent account and you've failed to uphold your end of the arrangements. So if you don't have the total amount by time we close today then we will be sending out the bailiffs."

Duce sighed and shook his head as he thought to himself "if it ain't one thing it's another." He looked off for a second, and then noticed his bank coming up.

"Okay, I'll send you the money by today, I just gotta make a few calls, and I'll call Y'all back when I'm sending it to you." Duce said as he pulled into his banks parking lot.

Duce hung up the phone and carefully backed into the parking spot. He put his car in park and took the keys out of the ignition. Out the corner of his eye he noticed a sexy beautiful brown skinned sista getting out of her car about to head into the bank. She was petite and very shapely with long black hair that draped down the back of her designer leather waist length coat. He immediately looked in the mirror to make sure that he was on point. He quickly got out of the car shutting the door behind him and then paced his self to meet up with her at the door.

"Hey, how you doing?" Duce asked as he smoothly greeted her, opening the door for her.

"I'm fine. Thank you for opening the door for me."

"Anytime for you, sexy."

"You probably say that to every pretty girl you meet." Devonah said as they walked over and got in line."

"Not at all baby, but what's your name?" Duce asked as he got in line behind her.

"Devonah. What's yours?"

"I'm Kevin, but everybody calls me Duce." He said as he extended his hand for a hand shake.

"Well it's nice to meet you Mr. Duce." She said with a slight smile as she shook his hand.

"It's nice to meet you too, sexy lady." He said as they got in line.

"Thank you. I like your glasses."

"Thank you baby. I try to stay stuntin." Duce said as he smiled and slightly adjusted his glasses.

"Oh you do it like that huh?" Devonah asked, thinking he may be a baller.

"I can show you better than I can tell you."

"Really? Oh okay."

"Why don't you let me treat you out and spoil you sometimes or do you got a man?"

"Yeah...I do but I'm about to be single soon anyway because I can't deal with drama."

Just as they were talking and filling out their transaction slips the bank teller behind the counter called out for the next person in line. Devonah stepped up to the counter to make her transaction and the bank teller just next to her called up Duce. He handed the clerk his withdrawal form and his driver's license, and she entered his information into the computer. After about forty-five seconds she looked up at Duce.

"Sir your account is seriously overdrawn by three-hundred and seventy- six dollars and fifty-five cents." The bank teller said very loudly causing others to look over at him.

"What? What are talking about?" Duce asked as he unconsciously gripped his front pockets and then glanced at Devonah to see if she was looking.

"Sir, it says here that your account is overdrawn by three-hundred and seventy-six dollars and fifty-five cents. You ought to know if your account is overdrawn or not. Now I can print you out an account summary all though you should already be receiving that in the mail." The bank teller said as she printed him out a summary and slid it through the slot of the bullet proof window.

"Why your fake, clown looking make up wearing ass putting my business out there to everybody?!" Duce asked, feeling embarrassed.

"Fake? Clown? Who are you calling a fake clown?" The bank teller asked, very appalled.

"Yeah, your fake ass looks like a damn clown. Your damn hair is fake, the back part look all silky and straight and the front edges look like hay and straw, your damn eyelashes so pasty and lanky looking I thought you was Snuffleupagus, plus you got enough foundation on your face to build a Hud House on." Duce insulted her as he snatched the account summary and walked away.

"Don't get mad at me because you're a low-life broke bum that can't manage your money right." The bank teller said as she gave him a nasty look.

Duce turned and yelled "Yeah, well at least I can manage to keep my face the same color as the rest of my body. It ain't Halloween!" Duce said, speaking on her foundation being a different color from her natural skin.

Duce walked out trying to catch up with Devonah. He noticed her in her car driving in his direction to exit the parking lot so he flagged her down. She stopped to make sure that she didn't hit him. He leaned and looked in the passenger window signaling her to role the window down. She rolled it down about an inch Peering at him with an irritated look on her face.

"What's up?" She asked with the car slightly moving giving him the hint that she was ready to go.

"Hey sexy, you gotta excuse what just happened in there, the lady was unprofessional and must've pulled up my father's account with his broke ass, because me and him got the same last name, you know. And I can tell you're ready to go because you're kind of driving real slow while I'm talking to you—" Duce said while peering through the barely cracked window while walking backwards as the car was moving.

"Okay, come on and say what you gotta say because I gotta go." Devonah impressed while sneering at him.

"Well I was like just wondering if you could go ahead and give me your number real quick so I can treat you out latter and show you a good time." Duce said as he whipped out his phone.

"Boy Bye! Get your broke ass away from my car!" Devonah said very loutish as she pulled off.

Duce stood up and looked at her as she was pulling off feeling low, and insulted.

"Good! I was just trying to be friends with your lonely looking ass! I ain't want you like that any damn way....Heffa!!!" Duce blurted out as he watched her stick the middle finger up at him out of the window.

Duce walked to his car, opened the door and got in.

"Stupid ass, clown looking bank teller gone mess it up for me...... Damn that girl was fine!" Duce yelled to his self as he tried starting his car to pull off.

The car wouldn't start all the way when he turned the key in the ignition.

"Damn, now the damn car want to act up right when it's freezing cold out here!"

He tried turning the key once again as he repeatedly mashed the gas pedal. He looked inside the glove compartment and grabbed the pliers. He pulled the hood release then got out off his car and walked to the front and lifted the hood. With no gloves on he took the pliers and tightened the nuts on the cold hard battery as tight as he could. In the process of doing so the pliers slipped and he whacked the shit out his hand on a cold ass piece of metal!

"Damn!!!!!" Duce yelled out, grabbing his hand in frustrating agony.

6

Pressure Bust The Pipes

6:12pm **Regina pressed the on** button on the salon stereo as she, Benita, Peaches, and De'Juan listened to the soulful sound of classic R&B while they cleaned up the place. Regina was wiping down the counter while talking on her phone. Benita and De'Juan were whipping down the hydraulic chairs and Peaches was cleaning the mirrors. Peaches sat the cloth she was using down on the station cleaning and walked to the back to use the restroom. She opened the door to the back room and stepped in shutting the door behind her. She walked over to her locker and grabbed the lock then turned the dial to put in the code to open it. She opened the door and took her purse out and sat it on the chair that was sitting next to her locker. She reached in and grabbed a slender brown and gold pocket book with a broken fastener. She took the money out of her pocket that she had made earlier and the money from her pocketbook and counted it together. Seven hundred and forty-six dollars she counted as she smiled thinking about how she was going to do some last minute shopping for her daughter. She couldn't hold her pee any longer so she tossed all the money in her purse and sat it on the chair real quick, because when you gotta go you gotta go. She darted into the restroom and shut the door behind her as her legs shimmied repetitively as she unfastened her pants, took them down and flopped down on the toilet.

In the mean time Duce had pulled up out front. He got out of his car still frustrated and worried about not wanting to get put out of his apartment. He stomped the snow off of his feet right in front of the door and walked in. "Hey Duce, thought you were done for the day?" Benita asked. "I am. I just came back up here to get something." Duce answered, trying not to look too stressed.

"Have you finished all of your Christmas

shopping?" De'Juan asked Duce as he continued wiping off the furniture.

"Yeah for the most part." Duce replied sort of dry.

"Okay...Don't say it so excitedly." De'Juan said sarcastically.

"Look, everybody ain't in the mood to play." Duce said as he glanced at him and kept stepping.

"First of all I ain't did nothing wrong to you so you can keep your attitude to your damn self." De'Juan replied with a dirty look.

Duce nonchalantly waived him off and walked over to Regina. Regina didn't actually see what had just happened but she sensed that there was some uneasiness there. She figured that something was troubling him as he approached her with a bleak written face.

"Everything thing okay?" Regina asked as she covered the mouth of the phone with her hand.

"Yeah, yeah everything's cool, I just need to holla at you in private." Duce answered.

"Okay give me a second to finish handling this business and I'll be right with you." Regina said as she got back to her call.

Duce walked to the back room and went inside. He shut the door behind him and went over to his locker. He took out his keys to open the lock on his locker but immediately looked to his left as he noticed out of his peripheral vision what he had been in dire need for.....money. He stuck his hand in Peaches purse, and took the money from her pocketbook. He heard someone at the door coming into the backroom so he hurried and tossed the money into his right pocket. He pretended like he was locking his lock as Benita walked into the back room.

"Hey Duce, Regina looking for you." Benita said as she walked to the cabinet and grabbed some paper towel.

"Alright, thanks." Duce replied as he walked up front thinking about what he was going to say to her.

Duce walked up front but really didn't want to engage in a long conversation with Regina. He tried to keep it quick and concise.

Peaches had just finished having her brief private conversation on the phone and walked out of the restroom, noticing Benita walking back up front. Peaches naturally looked in her purse and immediately became enraged when she noticed her money was gone. She got everyone's attention as she darted up front, slamming the door shut behind her and her eyes focused directly at Benita.

"Benita, did you go in my purse and take my money?" Peaches asked with a serious face and bucked eyes.

"Girl, don't play with me. I don't steal shit from nobody." Benita replied, looking dead at her.

"Okay, well who the fuck stole my money out my got damn purse?!" Peaches asked fiercely.

"Well it damn sho ain't me." Duce answered with a slightly guilt written face.

"When did you notice your money gone?" Regina asked, mind blown about what the hell was happening.

"I had just counted my money, set it in my purse, and went into the bathroom." Peaches answered emphatically.

"Well the only two people that has been back there since you've been back there is me and Duce, and I ain't touched nothing of yours. Y'all can all search me right now, I don't give damn because I ain't got nothing to hide." Benita impressed.

Peaches looked over at Duce with a mean scowl on her face and her head tilted to the side.

"Don't look at me, I ain't touched your shit! Now I'll holla at Y'all later." Duce said.

"Nall, don't nobody leave until we find this money." Regina said as she looked around at everybody.

"Look I ain't got shit." Duce said as he rabbit eared his pants pockets to make himself sound believable.

"Look, why don't both of Y'all just empty out every pocket Y'all got and we'll see if either one of Y'all have her money. Y'all were the only two back there." Regina said trying to get down to the truth.

"I done showed Y'all my pockets now I'm about to go." Duce said as he started to turn and walk out.

De'Juan was standing in back of Duce and just happened to notice a wad of money in his right jacket pocket.

"Oh yeah, what's this?" De'Juan asked as he snatched the wad of money out of Duces jacket pocket.

"Dog, give me my fuckin money." Duce said as he looked at De'Juan with his fist tightly bald.

"Not until we find out if it's yours or not." De'Juan said as he held it in his hand.

"I said give me my fuckin money you gay, homo ass bitch!" Duce blurted out as he threw a punch to knock De'Juan in his face.

De'Juan dodged Duce's punch and grabbed Duce's left wrist with his left hand, and threw him off balance as he mashed on the back of his left shoulder with his right hand, forcing him to the ground. De'Juan chicken winged Duce's arm behind him as he put his knee in his back so he couldn't move. Regina immediately walked over and picked the money up off of the floor.

"Yeah, well if that's so, you shole in the wrong position to be running your mouth." De'Juan replied sarcastically.

"How much money did you have?" Regina asked as she looked at Peaches.

"Seven hundred and forty-six." Peaches answered with a pissed look on her face.

Regina counted the money carefully, and pitifully shook her head as she looked at Duce.

"Seven Hundred and Forty-six dollars exactly. Why would you take her money, Duce?" Regina asked as she handed Peaches her money.

"Yeah, why would your low down punk ass go in my purse and take my money! Don't go in my shit!" Peaches yelled as she ran over to stomp Duce in the face.

Regina grabbed her and stopped her before she could do so and make matters worse.

"Man, let me up dude. All your weight stopping me from breathing." Dude barely said.

De'Juan lifted him up to his feet, and let him go. Duce couldn't look them in the eyes as he just sort of gazed at the floor. He knew he was wrong but his pride and arrogance would make any apology he said insincere.

".....My bad....." Duce said insincerely as he nonchalantly looked around the room.

Regina shook her head with disbelief written all over her face. She was disgusted with the bullshit apology that he gave them.

"Wow..." Regina uttered with a sneering smirk on her face.

With a slow cocky swagger Duce turned and walked to the door then opened it. Before he walked out he looked back.

"I was just trying to make you feel better by apologizing. I should've said nothing." Duce said with a sneered look on his face as he walked out leaving the door open.

"I oughtta-!" Peaches yelled as she charged at him before being grabbed by De'Juan.

"Calm down sweetie, let him go, he ain't even worth it." De'Juan stressed to peace the situation.

7

Christmas Eve

2:57pm Cognac unlocked her house door and opened it. She stomped the snow off of her feet onto the welcome mat and then stepped in. She shut the door behind her and took her shoes off and put on her house shoes. She walked over to the kitchen sink, sat her purse down and poured her a glass of water. She turned around and leaned back up against the counter, took a deep breath and shook her head in disbelief. She grabbed her cell phone out of her purse to call Regina, but decided not to then laid it down on the counter. She lowered her head and exhaled as she pondered upon the unfortunate news she received earlier. A few minutes passed and she heard a knock at the door. With curiosity written all over her face she wondered who could it be, and why they didn't call first before they came. She walked to the door and rose up on her tip toes to look through the peep hole. She sighed with frustration, wondering what the hell this nigga doing here. She opened the door and looked at him with a mean stank look on her face.

"You got a lot of fuckin nerve to be showing up at my door step after fuckin MY EX friend in MY HOUSE up in MY bed." Cognac expressed very grimly as she stood in the door looking at him.

"Can I come in and talk to you for a minute?" Marcello humbly asked.

Cognac just looked at him then shook her head because she couldn't believe that this soap opera type drama was happening to her.

"Yeah……come on in…I need to talk to you anyway." Cognac said as she opened the door further allowing him to step in.

Marcello took off his coat and hung it on the back of the kitchen chair and sat down.

"Uh uh, don't take your coat off, don't even think about trying to get comfortable up in here with your disrespectful ass." Cognac said as she walked over and leaned back up against the kitchen sink.

Marcello got up and put his coat back on and then slowly walked over to Cognac.

"That's close enough." She said as she put her hand up, palm forward.

Marcello stopped right there and he closed his eyes and shook his head.

"I know what I did was wrong, stupid, pathetic, and" Marcello said before being abruptly cut off.

"Mmmm Hmmm, yes you are wrong, stupid, pathetic and ridiculous, and immature. Go ahead, keep going." Cognac sarcastically added.

Marcello paused for a second till she finished venting.

"You finish?" He asked.

"Yeah I'm good. Go ahead and say what you were saying."

"Just to make a long story short, I apologize for the stupid thing I did. I wish I would've never done nothing stupid like that."

"I was a good woman to you. I had your back and I honored you. I cooked for you, washed your dirty ass clothes, made unrestricted love to you everyday not holding nothing back. And I know that tack head ass heffa ain't gone do half the things I did to intimately please you. I did the things that other men wish their women weren't afraid to do. And on top of that this braud is living off of child support, ain't even trying to work. She told me that the only reason she didn't want any of her four baby fathers to have equal custody rights and parenting time is because she rather have the money which is a sad reason to have legal custody over children. And you chose that over me? You thought the grass was greener but your vision was impaired, and now you see clearly that you was a fool."

"I guess I better be leaving." Marcello replied as he turned to head for the door.

"Hold on." Cognac said, making him look back at her.

"I gotta tell you something."

"Tell me what?" Marcello asked with a look of curiosity.

Marcello calmly walked back over to her to hear what she had to say. Cognac took a deep breath, looked down at the floor and then back up at him.

"Unfortunately I'm pregnant." Cognac said as she looked him dead in the eyes.

There was a brief moment of silence as Marcello stared at her with his mouth slightly opened.

"What do you mean you're pregnant?"

"I'm pregnant... with your baby...."

Marcello stood there gazing in disbelief with his mouth slightly moving as if he was trying to utter something, but was lost for words. He looked around with a hopeless look on his face.

"You can't have it." Marcello uttered pitifully.

"What? What do you mean I can't have it?"

"You shouldn't have it." Marcello said as he glanced at her then looked away.

"What the hell you mean I shouldn't have it, Marcello?" Cognac asked as she stood straight up.

Marcello took a deep breath and stood there unable to look her in the face. He waited a few seconds and finally uttered "I'm married." Cognac's body felt hollow and lifeless, not thinking this situation could get any worse.

"You're married? And you couldn't have told me in the beginning that you were married? Instead you kept it a secret, played me for my love and affection? I gave you my body and that which was sacred to me, and this is how I get rewarded?" Cognac asked with water filled eyes and a face filled with pure pain and hate.

"We are in the process of getting a divorce and I knew that you would look at it in the wrong way and not give us a chance if I had told you in the beginning." Marcello expressed sincerely.

"You know what? I truly understand that people can be so critical and quick to judge others that they scare someone from telling them the truth. But I never judged you or gave you that impression. You're a fuckin drug dealer with a real bleak future that only offers you a prison or death sentence unless you choose to do something better with yourself. I still stuck by your side, never judging you but believed in you and figured that you would leave that life alone and do better..... I hate you. Get the hell out of my house." Cognac yelled as she looked up at him with a face filled with resentment and pain.

With nothing to say Marcello turned and walked towards the door. As he opened the screen door he looked back and told Cognac that he loved her. He knew that his words fell upon deaf ears from Cognac's emotionless silence. So he left, calmly shutting the door behind him. Cognac walked over and sat down in her kitchen chair with her elbows upon her knees and her face in her palms, and cried.

8

Intimate Conversations FM 96.9

10:01PM 96.9 FM radio station phone lines had been ringing off the hook with callers calling in to speak on the hot relationship subject. Radio talk personalities Mrs. Sarah Langston and her special guest host Ms. Carmen Renae were just coming back from a brief intermission. They took their seats in the studio in front of the microphones and continued the conversation once the commercial went off.

"Hey what's going on Detroit? We are live here at FM 96.9 WDAV and I just want to say welcome to all the new listeners that have just tuned in. Tonight we have been blessed to have our very special guest host, and relationship specialist Ms. Carmen Renae and she has been giving out some seriously helpful advice. We're about to take the first caller. WDAV, go ahead with your question." Sarah Langston said.

"Hello, my name is Tania and I have a question for Carmen." Tania said.

"Go ahead with your question." Carmen said with a smile on her face.

"My boyfriend says that I am wrong because I search through his pants pockets, cell phone, and wallet sometimes. He says that I should trust him and stop violating him. It's causing a growing problem in our relationship, and I was wondering what I should do. Am I wrong for my actions?" Tania asked as she sniffed.

"First try not to cry Tania, it may not even be what you think it is. Let me ask you something. Has he ever cheated on you?" Carmen asked.

"No, I've never caught him with anyone."

"Do you suspect he's cheating on you?" Carmen asked as she crossed her legs.

"I don't know. I just constantly wonder in the back of my mind if he is out with someone else."

"When you search through his pockets and cell phone have you ever found any women's phone numbers?"

"No."

"What type of work does he do? Does he work around a lot of women?"

"He works at a place called CazTech, they make parts for the auto companies. And yes it is a lot of women that work there as well."

"Where do you work?" Carmen asked with an eyebrow raised.

"I work at the Mirage, it's a bar and grill."

"And what do you do there?"

"I'm a waitress."

"Have you ever cheated on him?"

"No."

"Sounds to me like you guys have something in common, you both work with the opposite sex. Let me ask you something before I share with you what I think. Do you really love this man?"

"Yes."

"Tania, no relationship is going to ever work without trust. It also will never work if you don't have reciprocity. You work around a lot of men every day, and you serve them.

I'm sure you wouldn't want your man falsely accusing you of cheating with someone where you work. You would want him to trust you. And if you have reciprocity you will trust him just as you want to be trusted. You cannot build a new house on an old foundation. Whatever toxic relationship that you experienced in the pass let it go and don't bring it to your current relationship because it will only poison the good thing you already have." Carmen stressed.

"Thank you so much. I needed that." Tania said while still sniffling.

"Y'all gone be alright, just stick with it and leave any past negativity in the past, and keep building your beautiful future with the man you're with."

"Okay, thank you Carmen, and thank you to Miss Sarah for always having an inspiring show." Tania said

"Hey, thank you Tania for being such a beautiful person. Keep loving, and never let no one from your past cause you to bury the love that God instilled in you." Sarah said with a pleasant smile.

"I wont."

"Okay Tania. Thanks for calling." Sarah said as she hung up and took the next caller.

"FM 96.9 WDAV, thanks for calling. Who am I speaking with?" Sarah asked as she greeted the caller.

A calm silence filled the airwaves as they waited for a second for the caller to speak.

"Hello, FM 96.9. Caller, are you there?" Sarah asked.

".....Yes, I'm sorry. I have a question."

"Okay, caller what's your name?" Sarah asked as she glanced at Carmen.

"...Anonymous."

"Okay, that's fine. Go ahead, what's your question?"

"Well, I'm sort of in a messed up position, and I don't know what to do. I was recently dating this guy that I really loved, and I came home the other day and I caught him having sex with one of my so-called friends in my bed. Of course I dealt with her and I put him out. Earlier today I went to the Doctor because I had been feeling cramps in my stomach and I found out that I was two months pregnant by him. Minutes after I got home from the doctor he popped up at my house unexpectedly. And ummmmmmmm, just to make a long story short, he told me to not have the baby because he was married."

"What?!" Sarah said as she looked at Carmen.

"Yes, he's married. I did not know that he was, he never wore a ring, he never mentioned anything about her, and we were basically together all the time."

"Wow." Carmen replied.

"So you never saw any signs or even suspected that he was with someone?" Sarah asked.

"No, because he was always with me, and when we weren't around each other we would be on the phone all day."

"So I suppose your question is what should a woman do if she found out that she was pregnant by a married man?" Sarah asked.

"Yes it is." Anonymous answered with a crackled voice, unable to hold back tears.

"Will this be your first child?" Carmen asked.

"No it wouldn't. I already have a son and I wasn't planning on having anymore kids, because I'm trying to get my life together. I don't believe in having abortions, and I feel like this whole situation is unfair to me, and I don't deserve none of this." Anonymous replied.

"And you don't think the father would want to be a part of the child's life?" Carmen asked.

"I really don't know. I mean should I tell his wife, or should I just say to hell with both of them and raise the child on my own?" Anonymous asked.

Carmen closed her eyes and pitifully shook her head, disheartened by such a heavy situation. Sarah also moved by the unfortunate circumstances and replied.

"Well first let me say that I respect your decision to not have an abortion because that is a human life inside of you. Secondly, I wouldn't take it upon myself to tell his wife because that is his responsibility. And trust me, she'll find out because if he has any decency he'll make sure that his child is a part of his life, and she'll either deal with it or leave him. But raising that child on your own should be a last option because a child needs a mother and father in their life."

"....Okay..." Anonymous slightly uttered.

"And most of all, pray. It will keep you strong as you embrace these trying times. You hear me?" Carmen asked.

"Yes." Anonymous replied.

"Okay, well you be strong, and take care." Sarah said as she deeply for the caller.

"Thank you." Anonymous said as she hung up.

9

Who The Fuck She Think I Am?!

The sound of steel weights clang with every rep as Marcello lied back on the weight bench at his house lifting two hundred pounds. He lifted with no problem as the bar banged him in the chest as he tossed it back up with ease. Each rep seemed to be fueled by his angered thoughts of Cognac. His boy, Andre who was working out with him stood along side just in case he needed him to grab the weights.

"I don't know who the fuck she think I am, but Ima get her fucking mind right." Marcello vowed to Andre.

"Damn dog, she got you going like that? Man, leave her ass alone, it's too many breezy's out here for you to be trippin over her" Andre said just as Marcello stopped lifting and sat it on top of the suspension brackets.

"MAN FUCK THEM BITCHES, I ain't worried about them right now. I got enough headaches. Why don't you hook me up and toss me two more plates on the bar so I can feel this shit." Marcello said, referring to the forty-five pound steel plates.

"Alright nigga, don't fuck yourself up trying to be Hercules while you're mad." Andre warned as he placed a forty-five pound weight on each side of the bar.

"Man fuck that, I got this." Marcello stressed.

Marcello inhaled and exhaled heavily as he murmured his frustrations and lifted. Thoughts of her being non-understanding and seeing somebody else was pissing him the fuck off. Veins surfaced by his temple the more reps he did. He sat the bar down secured on the suspension brackets then got up and immediately started punching the shit out of the punching bag that was hanging from the ceiling about five feet over from the weight bench. Andre was trippin in his mind as he watched Marcello take his rage out on the punching bag all over Cognac.

"I can't stand her stupid ass way of thinking! Talking that dumb shit about me being married, I tried to tell her stupid ass that shit is just on paper. The shit kept getting thrown out of court because we kept missing the dates, and it just never got finalized. That's it, that don't mean I was still with the bitch. Common sense will tell you that if I'm with your stupid ass every fucking day and she don't even call my phone that I wasn't with the bitch." Marcello said as continued pounding the bag.

"So Y'all broke up because she found out you were still married to your EX?" Andre asked.

"Nall, we broke up because she walked in and saw me fucking her girl. Damn!!!" Marcello blurted out as fiercely slapped a half drunken bottle of beer from off a table onto the floor making suds and glass splatter everywhere.

"Dog chill, man you slippin right now." Andre pointed out.

"Don't tell me to chill, I ain't even did shit yet." Marcello said as he grabbed two more bowling pen bottles of beer out of the case and tossed Andre one of them.

Andre caught his, then carefully twisted the cap off so the suds didn't rush up and took a chug. Marcello twisted the cap off of his and took a swallow.

"Dude, I just want you to look at yourself right now. You're sounding like an enraged killer. What did you expect if you were caught banging in her girl? And how did she catch you? Did she catch you over her girl house fucking her?" Andre asked.

"Naw, she came home and caught us at her place." Marcello confessed.

"Dog, don't tell me you were in your girl's bed fucking her friend. PLEASE TELL ME that's not what you're saying?" Andre asked, looking at him in disbelief.

"Yes nigga that's what I'm saying." Marcello admitted then sipped his beer and shook his head.

"Man you's a damn fool for that one. You better be glad she didn't kill yo ass. What the hell made you do some crazy shit like that?" Andre asked.

"Man, she shouldn't have kept having her girl always coming over smoking and getting high with us. My girl would be kissing me and grabbing my dick in front of her friend and shit. So one time her girl made a comment about she might want to join in on one of our sessions, because I guess it was getting her horny watching my girl grope on me. Hell, my girl never said shit about it and it made me wonder if my girl was down with something like that."

"How her friend look? She must look good?" Andre asked, all in to the story.

"HELL YEAH she look good." Marcello emphasized.

"She got a fat ass?" Andre asked.

"Like a fucking porno star." Marcello emphatically stressed.

"Damn that shit sound good! Alright finish telling me what happened." Andre said as he took another swig of his brew.

"So one day just before Christmas her girl stopped by to drop something off to her. I told her that Coney wasn't there so she handed me an envelope for her and asked me to give it to her, I said alright and she turned around and started walking away. I swear her ass was looking juicier than ever in these fitting ass jeans she was wearing but I didn't take it no further than just me looking. Right before I got ready to close the door she turned around and asked could she use the bathroom so I let her use it. I didn't think shit of it, she used the restroom, she came out, and as she was walking out she stopped and asked me when was me and my girl having another smoke session. I told her I didn't know and to ask Coney. She said Ima ask her about more than just the smoke session. I was like what more you gone ask her about and she was like that threesome. And then she tested my manhood by saying I might be scared of something like that anyway."

"And what you say?"

"I said I ain't scared of shit. And then her sexy ass walked over to me and squatted down in front of me and said "What if I was like this? You scared now ain't you?"

"And what you say?" Andre asked, taking a sip from an empty bottle of beer.

"I didn't say shit...I just looked at her. And then she started kissing and rubbing my dick through my pants. My dick was harder than a penitentiary brick in the winter time. Then she unzipped my pants and pulled my dick out and started sucking the shit out of my dick. I felt guilty about it at the time but hell, we was already in the act of sex, and it wasn't like I could change what already got started so I fucked the dog shit out her." Marcello said shaking his head.

Andre was in a trance just thinking about the shit.

"Man, now why can't that shit happen for me like that?" Andre asked sincerely.

"See your ass would do the same thing, and you up here talking shit about me." Marcello said.

"Only difference is I would've made my girl join in." Andre said humorously.

"Yeah well it didn't happen for me that way. She ended up beating her girl's ass. I tried to break it down to her how she kind of had something to do with it happening but her stupid attitude having ass just wouldn't listen...Then come to find out my girl pregnant by me." Marcello confessed as well.

"She pregnant by you, dog? Are you fucking crazy man?" Andre asked in disbelief.

"Hell yeah." Marcello uttered as he tilted the bottle up and finished the rest of his beer.

"Man your life is over." Andre said, being funny.

"Trust me, ain't shit over. She gone either do it my way or..." Marcello said and abruptly stopped talking then took out his cell phone and started pressing the keypad.

Andre was waiting on him to finish saying what he was saying and said "Do it your way or what?"

Marcello didn't answer he just kept pressing the touch screen on his phone.

"Dude, what are you doing?" Andre asked with an incredulous look on his face.

"Checking to see if she's at home." Marcello answered with his eyes fixated on the phone.

"You bout to call her? She ain't gone answer so how you gone find out?" Andre asked.

"I ain't calling her." Marcello replied.

"Okay then, how the hell are you gonna see if she's at home?" Andre asked with a puzzled look on his face.

Marcello looked over at him with a straight face and said "Satellite."

"Satellite?" Andre asked with an unbelievable look on his face.

"Yes nigga, I can see if her ride is parked in the drive way or if another dude car is there." Marcello expressed.

"Dude, you're going a bit too far with this, bro. You're officially going into stalk mode. You should stop before you see something you don't want to see and then you gone do something you regret." Andre said, trying to talk some sense into him.

"Trust me, I ain't gone regret shit.......she will." Marcello uttered sinisterly.

10

Christmas Surprise

11:15pm Cognac was asleep, and leaned over with her head resting on a couple of comfortable plush pillows stacked on the arm of her velvet black sectional couch. She awakened from her slumber, startled by a few knocks at her door. She took a deep breath and exhaled as she eased up off of the couch to go see who it was. She rose up on her tip toes and looked through the peep hole and saw that it was Regina. She rubbed her barely opened eyes as she opened the door.

"Dang Coney you had me worried about you. I've been calling, you ain't been answering so I came over here armed and dangerous." Regina said with a smile.

"Woman, you don't even have a gun to be armed and dangerous with." Cognac said as she let Regina in.

"Yeah, but I do got this pepper spray for that ass if someone was trying to mess with you. Nobody don't mess with my favorite cousin." Regina said as she reached in her purse and brandished the black pepper spray canister on her keychain.

"You have always been protective over me and that's why I love you, bay." Cognac replied as she hugged Regina.

Regina walked over to the sink and leaned up against the counter where she sat her purse down. Cognac leaned back against the counter just kitty-cornered of Regina.

"So, what's the verdict?" Regina asked as she looked up at Cognac all bright eyed.

"Pregnant." Cognac said reluctantly.

"Don't sound so un-enthused. Are you going to tell Marcello?"

"Sorry I don't sound so happy about it. And I did tell him, he popped up over here as soon as I walked in from the hospital." Cognac said as she shook her head while looking down.

"And, what did he say?"

"He told me not to have it."

"What? Why?" Regina asked, startled by the news she had just got.

Cognac snickered to herself and remained silent. Regina could sense that there was something more troubling then what Cognac was actually saying.

"Cognac, what's wrong? Why did he tell you not to have the baby?"

"Because he's married." Cognac answered with a plain face.

"Married?!" Regina asked with her mouth wide open.

"Yes you heard it right, married."

"What the hell? And you had no idea that he was married or involved?"

"Actually I didn't. It was as big of a shock to me as it is to you. But I don't want to talk about it right now because I've been beating myself up about it all day."

Regina walked over and gave her a hug.

"Well, you ain't gone be alone in this because I'm going to be here for you and the baby. Matter of fact come get out of the house with me, uncle Gary is at home cooking Christmas dinner. He invited us over, and that's why I was calling you to see if you wanted to go over there. A few of our family members will be there."

"You're going to drive way to the eastside with all that snow on the ground like that?" Cognac asked as she looked out of the window.

"Girl, I'll catch the bus over there right now just so I can taste test some of Uncle Gary's cooking. His fat butt can throw down." Regina said hilariously.

"He cooks like that?" Cognac asked with an eyebrow raised.

"Girl, that man cooks better than four fat Alabama grandma's in their prime."

"Well, I need to get out anyway, and I wouldn't mind tasting some good food right now. Let me go change clothes." Cognac said as she headed upstairs.

Cognac changed her clothes, and grabbed her purse then she and Regina headed out the door. They both got in Regina's car and headed over to Uncle Gary's house. After about twenty-five minutes of driving they finally arrived and parked in front of the house next door. They got out of the car and walked up to the house, and you could see smoke coming up from the barrel styled barbecue pit. Uncle Gary had walked out of the back door and over to the grill. He lifted the lid on the grill then dipped the basting brush into the special sauce that he made and started stroking the sauce onto the two juicy turkeys he had on the grill.

"Hey Uncle Gary." Regina said as she and Cognac walked into the back yard.

Uncle Gary turned around with a big smile on his face.

"Hey, how are my two beautiful little nieces doing? Merry Christmas!" Uncle Gary said as he opened his arms and hugged them both.

"Merry Christmas, Uncle Gary." Regina said as she kissed him on the cheek.

"Merry Christmas, Uncle Gary." Cognac said as she kissed him on the cheek as well.

"Dang, Uncle Gary you got it going on over here." Regina said as she looked at him finish basting the turkeys.

"I shole know who to call when I need a personal chef or some recipes or something." Cognac said while smiling as she watched Uncle Gary slather the glaze onto the browning turkey.

"Hey lets go in the house so Y'all can see the rest of the family. Your Aunt Marian is in there with her grand kids, your Uncle Calvin is in there with your Aunt Martha. Your Aunt Maxine is running around here somewhere. Come on lets go inside." Uncle Gary said as he shut the lid on the grill and headed into the house.

The house was smelling like straight up soul food as soon as you walked through the door. People were all in the cluttered kitchen. Food, mixing bowls, cooking utensils were laid out everywhere. Everyone was happy to see Regina, and Cognac as they stepped in the house. Aunt Marion was sitting in a chair just across from the door. Regina walked over and hugged her.

"Hey Regina, you are looking fabulous. You have grown to be such a fine sista, Mmmmm. I remember when I was a fly diva like yourself back in my day." Aunt Marian said as she smiled at Regina.

Aunt Maxine walked up to Cognac as she stepped in and hugged her. She held her hand as she stepped back and looked at her body.

"Rachelle too, look at this brick house right here. Rachelle got one of them stripper girl bodies."

"Auntie!" Cognac blurted out, shocked from Aunt Maxine's remarks.

"Hey I'm just saying, It looks good girl don't get me wrong. It just takes you two minutes for the rest of your booty to get in the door after you done stepped in." Aunt Maxine said jokingly.

"You are something else, Auntie." Cognac said as she smiled and walked over and hugged everyone else.

"Y'all ain't playing in this kitchen I see." Regina said as she looked at all the delicious food that was being prepared for the Christmas feast tomorrow at noon.

"Naw, you know I don't play when it comes to this kitchen. Can't you tell?" Uncle Gary said as he looked down at his self.

Regina shook her head and smiled at Uncle Gary's remarks. Gary had been throwing down on the food all night, and was finishing up his deserts. Strawberry cheese cake, apple pie, sweet potato pie, and a delicious lemon cake were laid out atop the counter. Gary's wife, Maxine convinced him into letting the grandchildren open their gifts at midnight. Gary couldn't wait to take those juicy golden birds off the grill so he told them to wait on him while he went to see if the turkeys were finished. When he walked outside he was confused because he didn't remember leaving the lid to the grill up. Then he noticed that one of the turkeys was missing and immediately looked around. He looked up the driveway and noticed a shabby looking man in raggedy clothes running away with his turkey in his arm.

"GIVE ME BACK MY DAMN TURKEY, YOU DAMN TURKEY THIEF!!!!" Uncle Gary said as he gave chase.

Everyone inside heard the yelling and ran outside to see what the hell was going on. They darted up to the front of the house and saw Uncle Gary chasing some dude up the street, so they gave chase as well. Gary's legs were getting tired as hell from being out of shape and the fact that he was running through snow. The hungry thief was taking bites of the turkey and continuously glancing back to make sure that Gary couldn't catch him. After chasing him about two blocks

Gary's Asthma became a factor. He became very fatigued so he started slowing up.

"IMA KICK YO ASS NEXT TIME I SEE YOU, YOU DAMN TURKEY THIEF!!!" Gary yelled as he raised his tightly balled fat fist up in the air.

Gary bent over breathing heavily and rested his hands on his knees. Regina, Cognac and some of their other cousins caught up to him.

"Uncle Gary, you okay?" Regina asked as she placed her hand on his back.

"Nall, I ain't okay. Ima kick sparks out his ass if I see him again." Uncle Gary said as he shook his head.

"Uncle Gary, you don't even talk like this." Regina said after being surprised by her Uncle choice of language.

"I know, you're right, sweetie. Thank you for keeping me focused. Please forgive me father God for my mouth is foul and my thoughts are wretched." Gary asked as he glanced up in the sky.

"Yeah, don't let it get to you it was just a turkey, Uncle Gary. It's going to be okay." Cognac said trying to ease the moment.

"Yeah, but it was my turkey though. Ohhhh Lawd if I see him again it's gone be a whole lot of crying and flower buying around this Mutha!" Uncle Gary sighed.

"Uncle Gary, I'll buy you another turkey. Don't be sad." Regina insisted.

"You just don't understand how a chef feels when it comes to cooking. All the preparation it takes to make the food. All the marinade and the S A U C E I basted on that turkey. A real chef doesn't just cook the food, but becomes one with the food, puts his LOVE into the food, and does it with passion." Uncle Gary sincerely emphasized.

"Dang Uncle Gary, the way you described that food sounds like you and that turkey needed to get a bottle of wine and room at a hotel." Cognac said being sarcastic.

"Very funny." Uncle Gary replied.

"Well I know one thing. It's cold out here and I'm ready to get back to the house where I can feel some heat." Regina impressed as her mouth shivered from being cold.

"I don't know what's wrong with Y'all, but I ain't cold." Uncle Gary said.

"Well we ain't gone speak on why you ain't cold, but my feet freezing!" Cognac replied, thinking to herself that he wasn't cold because he was fat.

They walked fast and made it back to the house. They stumped the snow off of their feet as they walked into the house. Everybody looked at them wondering what happened and started asking them questions.

"How in the hell do you let someone steal a hot ass turkey out a hot ass barbeque pit? What kind of cook is you, getting punked for a turkey." Leroy, Gary's older brother asked.

"Ain't nobody get punked for no turkey. Why don't you shut up with them big teeth in your mouth looking like dinosaur partials?" Gary sarcastically replied.

"Leroy, don't talk to your brother like that, he just ran two blocks chasing a thief through the snow for a turkey." Marian said to her husband, Leroy.

"Chasing? His fat ass wasn't chasing nobody. That man left him in the dust like Barry Sanders on Thanksgiving Day. Now what he was chasing was the damn smell of that turkey." Leroy replied sarcastically.

"I may be fat but at least I can see straight. The lenses in your glasses so damn thick I thought you had on prescription fiber glasses." Gary retorted.

"Yeah well at least I could catch a man that stole my turkey." Leroy said.

"You know Gary got bad knee caps. Now leave him alone." Marian said.

"Those are no longer knee caps. When you are that fat those are what you call hub caps." Leroy replied.

Marion, and Leroy's oldest son, Leroy Jr. was off to the side shaking his head at his dad and uncle cap on each other. He aligned some wine glasses that Regina had sat out along side of a bottle of Moet if anyone wanted to partake. He caught everyone's attention as he popped the cork off. He poured everyone a drink and passed them around to those who wanted some.

"I'd like to propose a toast." Leroy junior said as he looked around at everyone.

"Well, speaking of toast, I wonder what toast play for in the lottery." Leroy senior said as he looked around then held his glass up.

"Uh, what does shut the hell up play for? I'll damn sho drank to that." Gary replied as he held his glass up.

"Okay…lets toast to shutting the hell up."
Leroy junior said sarcastically as he held his
glass up.

Everyone in the room held their glasses
up and in unison said "Cheers!"

11

Xmas Party

6:34pm Regina and some of her friends were chillin in her basement after having some good Christmas dinner that Uncle Gary cooked. Regina, Benita, Peaches, Cynthia and her man Cedric were sharing some alcoholic drinks for the holiday, and having some good conversation. Cognac didn't drink due to her being pregnant. The ambiance in her wood grained finished basement was admirable; decorated with beautiful pain'tings and statues. Cedric and Cynthia were having a slightly testy conversation as they uttered amongst themselves and did their best version of keeping their composure. They say that when you get drink the truth comes out, well... everyone's cups were damn near empty and the conversation had just got a little juicier.

"Okay, okay, okay I got a question, check this out. And you gotta be truthful with your answer. If it's okay for a woman who is in a relationship to accept a drink from another man then is okay for her man to buy another woman a drink?" Cedric asked with a slightly slurred speech as he sipped his drink.

"Why are you putting all our business out in the street?" Cynthia asked him with a serious sneered look on her face.

"I'm not putting our business out in the streets, you are. For all they knew I was just asking a simple question." Cedric replied.

"I'm not the one that asked the damn question." Cynthia replied.

"Yeah but you the one that did it, and you think that shit is okay, and I want to know if other people think this is wrong to do." Cedric stressed as he glanced around the room and looked back at Cynthia.

"Don't be putting me on the damn spot." Cynthia replied very angered.

"Look, Y'all calm down, it's the holiday." Regina added trying to calm the situation.

"What's wrong with her accepting a drink that someone sent her? She's not sleeping with him." Benita said.

"Nothing, if it ain't nothing wrong with her man buying another woman a drink." Cedric replied.

"Yes it is very wrong for the man to buy another woman drinks. That's absolute disrespect, and violating the relationship." Peaches added.

"Don't add to the fire, Peaches." Regina asked.

"Thank you, Peaches." Cynthia said as she nodded her head with her lips pruned.

"So Peaches, you mean to tell me that it's okay for a woman to entertain a man by accepting drinks from him even if her man doesn't approve of it, but it's wrong for him to entertain another woman and buy her a drink?" Cedric asked in disbelief as he looked at Peaches.

"She didn't ask for the drink, it was sent to her. So why does that make her wrong?" Peaches asked.

"She's entertaining him by accepting the drink instead of exercising adequacy and respecting the fact that she doesn't want her man entertaining another woman and buying her drinks." Cedric replied.

"Yeah, but what's your intent behind buying her the drink? That's what makes it wrong." Cynthia impressed.

"So are you saying that men have some type of sexual intent when he buys a woman a drink?" Cedric asked.

"If it's a strange man that I don't know at the end of the bar and he sends me a drink that means he must 1.) Like what he sees and wants me to know it. 2.) He wants some conversation from me and wants to get to know me and see if I'm single or not. And 3.) If in fact I am in a relationship, how serious it is and if I'll creep and give up the booty on the low. That's a man's intentions when he buys her a drink." Peaches stressed.

"So you think a man should be okay if his woman accepts a drink from another man if she already knows that these are a man's intensions behind it? I don't think so, respect is a two way street. So if you don't want your man violating your wishes then don't violate his. Stop being cheap and buy your own damn drink. And if you don't have the money then get it from your man before you go, and if neither one of you have it then you don't need to be at the bar or the club in the first place." Cedric said very eloquently.

"Now I have to say I agree with Cedric on that. Respect is a two way street and if your relationship is what's most important then perhaps it would be best to just buy your own drinks when you are in a relationship." Regina added trying to spark a sense of balance to the conversation.

"Whatever, I say to each it's own. That's how I feel about it." Cynthia said very irritated.

"And it's because of that childish, irrational way of looking at it you got another person in the damn picture now." Cedric said firmly as he looked Cynthia in the eyes.

An uncomfortable silence filled the room as everyone looked on as Cynthia speechlessly stared at Cedric for a brief moment. They wondered to themselves if Cedric knew about Damon after the remarks he had made.

"What the hell are you talking about?" Cynthia asked as she regained her composer.

"You know exactly what the hell I'm talking about. Perhaps this explains why I found a couple of condoms in the car that wasn't mines and why you didn't answer the phone when I was calling you but you were on the phone when you pulled up to the house, Cynthia. Explain that." Cedric said as he reached in his back pocket and pulled out one of the condoms he found and tossed it on the floor next to Cynthia.

"Okay, its Christmas, and we're about to enjoy it. You two love birds just need a little counseling, that's all." Regina said trying to calm the situation.

"Counseling? Right." Cedric said as he chuckled sarcastically and took another sip of his drink, and shook his head.

Cynthia was embarrassed as she got up and put her coat on.

"For one, those are not my condoms, now I'm ready to go." Cynthia said as she buttoned her coat.

"Oh, I guess the condom fairy just mysteriously put them in your car, huh? Oh wait a minute one of your girl friends made a mistake and dropped them there, huh?" Cedric said very sarcastic as he got up and put on his coat.

"I don't know how they got there or who they belong to, all I know is they ain't mines." Cynthia stressed, lying through her teeth.

"You are such a fuckin liar, and full of shit." Cedric replied.

"Come on Y'all, calm down and try to enjoy the Christmas holiday." Regina asked.

"I'm sorry Gina, Ima just get up out of here because he trippin." Cynthia said as she hugged Regina.

"Whatever, you trippin if you keep thinking Ima keep accepting your bullshit." Cedric said as he grabbed his coat and put it on.

"Whatever, you don't have to talk about our business in front of people." Cynthia retorted.

"Like I said, they thought that it was just a random question until you said something." Cedric replied as he and Cynthia got ready to leave.

Cynthia and Cedric hugged everybody then walked up the staircase and out of the side door.

"Call me and let me know that you guys made it to your destination safely, and Merry

Christmas." Regina said to them as they shut the door behind them.

Regina sighed as she ran her fingers through her hair then turned around and walked over to her bar, grabbed her drink and took a sip.

"I think Cedric knows about Damon." Benita said as she glanced at Regina and shook her head.

"I don't know but that's why I tell her to stop playing with that man's heart. That stuff sparks domestic violence. I mean, is accepting a drink from someone that important if it's causing a problem at home." Regina replied.

"I don't know about Y'all but I'm about to find out what relationships, and drama play for in the lottery." Cognac said as she stood up to stretch after sitting down for so long.

Immediately Cognac bent over and grabbed onto the arm of the couch while holding her stomach after feeling some very sharp pains. Regina and Peaches rushed over to her as everyone else stopped what they were doing and looked on hoping that she is okay.

"Coney, are you okay?" Regina asked sincerely as she placed her hand on her back.

Cognac tightened her lips, squinted her eyes and breathed in very slowly as she stood up straight.

"Yeah, yeah I'm okay." Cognac slowly uttered.

"Are you sure? You got me worried." Regina replied.

"I'm cool, I just need to chill for a minute." Cognac said as she sat back down and stayed still.

12

OBSESSION

2:45pm the day after Christmas Cognac carried a few bags in her hand as she walked out of the department store. She returned the items that she had bought Marcello, and purchased a few things for herself and her son, Eric. Her every move was being scoped from across the parking lot. A well groomed man approached her as she got ready to put her bags in her car.

"Excuse me sweetie. How are you doing? I'm have a new years eve Ball that I'm throwing called the Chocolate and Cream Ball, you ought to come." Demarco said as he handed her a flyer.

Cognac looked at the flyer and recognized the sponsors who had promoted another off the hook party in the past.

"Oh I remember B&J from another party they promoted long time ago, it was off the hook." Cognac said as she looked back at him.

"Well, you see what type of parties we do. Why don't you come through? If you ask for me at the door I'll hook you and your girls up. Y'all can get in on me." Demarco impressed.

Okay, but you ain't even gone remember me." Cognac said sort of coy.

Demarco looked her up and down and said "Trust me, there's no way I'm going to forget your fine ass. Matter of fact you take my card and call me when you coming." Demarco said as he reached in his inner jacket pocket and pulled out one of his business cards and handed it to her.

Cognac looked at his card and asked "Demarco, huh?"

"That's me baby, the one and only."

"Okay Mr. Demarco I might just take you up on that offer." Cognac said as she put his card in her purse.

"Trust me you'll be glad you came." Demarco said as he slightly started easing towards his car.

"Okay, well it was nice to meet you." Cognac said as she hit the trunk unlock button on her key remote.

"Okay, it was nice to meet you to Miss....." Demarco said, not knowing what to call her.

"Cognac, my name is Rachelle but everybody calls me Cognac." Cognac said.

"Cognac, that's sexy. I like that. Well alright Cognac hopefully I hear from you, Ma." Demarco said.

"We'll see." Cognac said as she smiled then turned to put her bags in her trunk.

Demarco walked to his flashy rimmed up Chevy Caprice with tented windows. He opened the door then got in and started the car. Immediately his sounds started banging. It sounded like the screws and bolts in his trunk were going to rattle loose and fall open. He backed up and turned out. He eased back a little more and rolled his window down.

"You be safe out here, sexy."

"Thank you. You too."

Demarco cranked his sounds back up and pulled off. Cognac finished putting her bags in her trunk. She didn't pay attention to the car that was subtly easing up the lane she was parked in, and stopped right behind her.

"Sup Coney?"

Cognac turned around startled, and in disbelief that she's being scrutinized.

"Don't be sneaking up on me like that. What are you doing here anyway, Marcello?" Cognac asked as her chest panted in and out.

"I'm sorry baby, I didn't mean no harm." Marcello said as he put his car in park and got out.

"Marcello, why are you getting out of your car?" Cognac asked as she took a deep frustrating breath.

"I need to talk to you." Marcello said as he approached her.

"There's nothing to talk about, Marcello." Cognac said as she closed her trunk and started walking around to the driver's side door.

"Yes it is." Marcello said as he walked up on her and pressed his hand against the car door so that it wouldn't open.

"Can you please move your hand off of the door?" Cognac asked as she looked up in the air very discombobulated.

Men-Tal

"No. Can you please talk to me first?" Marcello replied.

"GO TALK TO YOUR WIFE, GO TALK TO TAMARA, CAUSE I AIN'T GOT NOTHING TO SAY!" Cognac said stressfully.

"She is not my wife! You are my wife!" Marcello said as he looked her in her eyes.

"NO I ain't yo damn wife, now move!" Cognac yelled as she grabbed his hand and tried to shove him back so she could open her car door.

"Look, calm yo ass down!" Marcello said as he grabbed her by her jaw and held her back up against the car.

Cognac tussled with him, trying to get his hand off of her. The veins surfaced in his hand as his grip tightened. A few people from a far off looked on but didn't want to get involved.

"Get your hands off of me!" Cognac managed to murmur out of her tightly cuffed mouth as she gripped his arm, sinking her nails into his skin.

"Calm your ass down and I will." Marcello said firmly.

"Leave me the fuck alone!" Cognac stressed.

"Who the fuck was that dude you was just talking to?"

"That ain't none of your business!"

"We just broke up a couple days ago, and you hollering at niggas already?!"

"Ain't nobody hollering at nobody now get your fucking hands off of my face!" Cognac murmured exhaustedly.

"Oh yeah, then what the hell was Y'all talking about?"

"It ain't none of your fuckin business!"

"It is my muthafuckin business!"

All while they were arguing and tussling the police that patrolled the mall had noticed the incident taking place. They whipped over to the heated situation and jumped out of the patrol car with their guns drawn.

"Sir, step away from her, place your hands behind your head and back away slowly!" Officer Clark yelled as he steadily aimed his weapon at Marcello.

Marcello complied with the officers and Cognac yanked his hand off of her face. With a steady angered stare into Cognac's eyes Marcello slowly placed his hands behind his head and interlocked his fingers, and then eased back.

The officers immediately ran over and cuffed him.

"This ain't over." Marcello uttered to Cognac as the officers pulled him away and then placed him in the back seat of the squad car.

One of the officers walked over to make sure Cognac was okay.

"Mam, are you okay?" Officer Davis asked.

"Yes I am." Cognac replied.

The officer asked Cognac to elaborate on what happened as he wrote everything down that she was saying. The situation was calmed and everything was back to normal. The police officer got into Marcello's car and pulled it up so Cognac could leave. Cognac took a deep breath, got in her car and pulled off.

13

December 27, 2010

11:37am **Essential Beauty Salon** was back in business after a very lively Christmas holiday. The scent of hot combs and curling irons was in the air. Quick weaves and sew-ins were being done as people could hardly wait to look sexy and fly for the New Years Eve parties they planned on attending. Just outside in front of the Salon was a young lady in her mid twenties walking by with her two children. She was pushing her two year old in a baby stroller and her five year old was straggling behind them carrying a half gallon of milk. She looked back at her daughter who was having a hard time and lashed out at her.

"Damn, can you hurry your slow ass up?!!! I don't have all fucking day! I got shit to do." The immature woman said as she grabbed her daughter by the sleeve of her jacket and yanked her forward, causing her to drop the milk.

"Sorry mommy." The little daughter said sincerely.

"Damn! Now you done bust the fucking milk! Come on!" The deadbeat mother said as she started pushing the stroller.

"I'm sorry mommy, I'll pick it up." She said trying to please her mom.

"You're little ass done busted the damn milk! Leave it there and come on!" The deadbeat mom said to her daughter as she reached back and grabbed her by the arm.

Regina walked outside and grabbed the grocery bag with the milk inside it and lifted it up. With milk dripping from the bag, she looked at the deadbeat mother with a heart filled with disgust.

"Excuse me." Regina said causing the deadbeat mom to look back.

"You talking to me?" The deadbeat mom asked as she turned around pointing to herself.

"Yes. Next time can you please pick up your trash and throw it in the trash can?"

Regina asked as she walked over and tossed the milk into the trash can.

"I'm sorry." The little daughter replied politely.

"Don't be apologizing to her! You don't even know her! Get yo ass over here!" The deadbeat Mom said as she snatched the little girl by the arm.

"You are a poor example of a mother." Regina said as she grew angry from the way the mother was treating the little girl.

"Fuck you! You don't tell me how to raise my fuckin kids!" The deadbeat mom said fiercely.

"Because you have your children with you I won't act a fool on you." Regina replied as humble as she could for sake of her children. "You feeling frogish?! Leap then! Leap muthafucka!" The deadbeat momma said, throwing her hands up looking all ignorant and hood ratish.

Regina looked at the little girl, and decided to be a respectable example for her as she was looking back and forth between Regina and her Mom. Regina made eye contact with the little girl and smiled.

"God bless you, sweetie." Regina said to

the little girl as she smiled and walked back inside the salon.

The little girl waived bye to Regina with a smile on her face. The Momma was pissed after seeing her daughter wave good bye to Regina.

"Don't speak to that bitch! Bring yo little ass on and let's go!" The deadbeat Mom yelled at her child as they turned and walked to their unfit home.

Regina walked back into the salon, heated as she shook her head while trying to keep her composure. There was an uneasy stir of choice words for the deadbeat Mom and how she treated her daughter. A slight smirk appeared on Regina's disgusted face as she allowed herself to exhale a little before she exploded.

"It literally took every bit of goodness in my body, and the respect that I had for that little girl for me not to have whooped her Momma's ass." Regina impressed as she walked back to station and sat down in her hydraulic chair sort of exhausted.

"I know how you feel. I had to catch myself before I came out there and started stomping her behind like a damn River

Dance." Peaches added as she did her clients hair.

"I don't want anybody to lose their kids but that type of abuse makes you wanna call Child Protective Services on these unfit parents." Benita stressed as she was doing a lace front wig hair-do for her client.

"Heck yeah! You have to be the most pathetic parent ever if you can just ruthlessly cuss your children the hell out like they're just nothing; all because she was walking slow because she was carrying the milk." Peaches stressed.

"Now wait a minute. I'm sure some of us if not all of us have cussed out our kids at some point in time for getting on our damn nerves." Benita's client voiced with a facial expression that screamed keep it real.

"I'm sorry sweetie, I don't know about you but I would never talk to my kids like that. I be hearing these parents dogging their kids out something scandalous, but they will never talk to their friends like that. But they will morally degrade their children, who they are supposed to love more than anybody." Peaches stressed a very convicting point.

"Right! But check this out. I just want to share a different point of view on this serious subject, and it might make you look at things a tad bit different about how you talk to people especially children. The word cuss derived from the word curse. People curse people all the time and don't even recognize it. I don't know if Y'all heard about the little thirteen year old boy from Dallas Texas that hung himself two weeks ago, but it was reported that when police found him they also found a suicide note that he wrote just before taking his own life stating that his mother cursed him all of his life calling him stupid ass, dumb ass and it made him feel that he couldn't do anything right. He wasn't confident with anything he did so he decided he didn't want to live anymore and hung himself." Regina expressed.

"That is so deep. That's why I try to keep excellent communication with my kids. If they do something wrong I just put them on time out." Peaches client said with a proud face.

"Timeout? Girl bye! God ain't never said nothing about no timeout. Timeout is only necessary when the parent needs to take a break in between ass whoopings. God said if you spare the rod you spoil the child. First, Ima kindly ask the beautiful children to calm down because they're getting on my nerves. If they don't calm down then I go to plan B, and Ima give em the look with some seriousness in my voice, a stick in my hand and say I said sit Y'all asses down! If that don't work then we will go to plan C." Benita said as she simply kept doing her clients hair.

Everybody kept looking at Benita waiting on her to say something more.

"Okay, what is plan C?" Regina asked with a smirk on her face.

"Plan C is when I go visit them in the hospital, and show em love and support on their road to recovery." Benita said.

Everyone busted out laughing at Benita's hilarious methods, but one by one they forgot about their conversation when they noticed the brown skinned brotha with a well trimmed goatee pull up in front of the salon.

"Girl I swear if he's coming in here and selling some of them urban fiction novels or something, I'll buy ten of them right now." Benita said as she kept glancing outside at him.

"Benita, you don't even read novels." Regina said sarcastically.

"That's not the point. He fine, sexy so that automatically qualifies you to get some shit bought if you selling something." Benita replied.

The guy got out of the car with a spiffy looking button up shirt, Sean Jean blue jeans and some dress shoes. He shut the car door, and headed to the salon. The ladies uttered things to the person next to them or just silently scoped as Mr. Eye Candy walked inside. Regina walked up and greeted the brotha with a firm handshake, and a smile.

"Are you Mr. Antonio?" Regina politely asked.

"Yes I am. And you must be Regina?" Antonio asked.

"Yes Sir. When are you trying to start?" Regina asked.

"Hey, I could start tomorrow actually." Antonio replied with slight smile.

In the mean time Peaches was walking up, coming from the back room. She was looking down at her cell phone, sending a text message. She was surprised when she looked up and saw a familiar face.

"Tony? What you doing here?" Peaches asked, pausing for a second with a slight smile on her face.

"Hey, wsup Peach? I'm supposed to start work here tomorrow." Antonio replied with a smile on his face as well.

"Wwoowww." Peaches said in disbelief.

"Y'all two know each, know each other?" Regina asked as she looked at both of them.

"Yeah something like that. We've met before." Peaches said, trying not to be too obvious.

"Okay, well just sit in one of these chairs over here and I'll be right back. I just need to go over a few stipulations with you." Regina said as she walked into the back room.

Up front the ladies asked Peaches how she knew the handsome guy, Antonio. Peaches knew that those gossiping hens would love to hear some live, juicy freaked out stories so that they can chit chat amongst themselves and hate. She kept it bleak and to the point, they're just friends that met a little while ago, and that was that. Regina met back with Antonio and went over a few things. With plans of returning tomorrow and starting work, Antonio parted ways with

Regina and walked towards the front door to leave. Scrutinized as he walked passed everyone getting ready to exit he looked at Peaches who was finishing up her clients hair.

"See you later, Peaches." Antonio said.

"See you tomorrow." Peaches said as she tried to hold in her smile so she turned around like she was looking for something.

Once Antonio shut the door behind him the remarks and comments came out. They playfully teased Peaches about Antonio, and how they sensed some type of connection. Peaches vaguely smirked but most of all she kept a straight face. Hey, anything you say can be used against you... Silence is golden under the innocent until proven guilty rule.

14

Healthy Conversation

2:57pm, Mrs. Sarah Langston drove westward up Schoolcraft Rd in her silver BMW on her way to her three o'clock appointment. She took a sip of her McDonalds coffee as her GPS prompted her to make a right turn on Greenview St. She peered at each house on the right hand side looking for the address until she finally found it. She pulled in front of the house, and parked. Inside, Cedric and Cynthia were sitting at his dining-room table having a peppery discussion about their relationship issues. Cynthia was trying her best to bring up irrelevant past issues about Cedric because he had a seriously incriminating accusation about her cheating. Cynthia was playing the innocent until proven guilty role until she got caught, and that she had no plans of doing. So to get him off of her head she would irrationally lash out at him the closer he got to prying the truth out of her. The doorbell rang, and they immediately tried to lower their voices so they would not to be heard.

"See that's your problem right there. When you have something to say to me you want me to respect you and listen to every word coming out of your mouth without interruption, but when I reply to something you say or voice my opinion about something you rudely cut me off before I finish, and that's what I be trying to--." Cedric stressed in a low tone as Cynthia cut him off.

"You be cutting me off too." Cynthia retorted immediately.

"No I don't, I let you speak, and then I respond after you finish. But you, you never let nobody finish saying--" Cedric said as he was cut off again.

"Yes you do!" Cynthia retorted again.

"Can you ever be rational and just have a cordial conversation without being over emotional and ridiculous with it?" Cedric asked.

"Why do I gotta be irrational just because I don't like something and I speak on it?" Cynthia asked.

"It's irrational because you never know how to wait your turn or talk peacefully without getting an attitude, or responding in a nasty manner. Plus whenever we do have a discussion you never can stick to the subject." Cedric stressed.

"You always trying to tell somebody how to talk." Cynthia stressed.

"Alright look lets chill for now, Mrs. Langston's at the door." Cedric said, trying to relax the situation.

"Just open the door, always trying to act like you perfect." Cynthia uttered.

"Look, chill out with all that. You and these damn attitudes." Cedric said with a slightly pissed look on his face before he opened the door with a smile.

Cedric and Cynthia had pleasant smiles written on their faces as they opened the door and greeted here. Sarah heard them mumbling on the other side and just looked at them both, thinking to herself yeah right, keep it real.

"I was starting to think I was at the wrong house or something." Sarah said as she stomped the snow off of her black designer boots.

"OOH NO, You're definitely at the right place. I need some help." Cedric said sarcastically as Sarah stepped inside.

"Please, if anything I'm the one in need of help because you driving me crazy. Anyway, how you doing Mrs. Langston? Thanks for coming by." Cynthia said as she hugged her, and kissed her on the cheek.

"Oh it's my pleasure to help two beautiful young people."

"Can I hang your coat up for you?" Cedric asked.

"Yes please, that would be nice." Sarah replied.

Cedric helped her take her coat off and he hung it up in the guest closet. Sarah followed Cynthia into the dining room and sat at the table.

"Can I get you anything to drink, bottled water, pop, milk, or juice?" Cynthia politely asked.

"Bottled water would be fine." Sarah replied.

Cynthia got up and walked into the kitchen as Cedric came in the room and sat down at the table. Cynthia returned and handed Sarah her water.

"Thank you kindly." Sarah said as she twisted the cap off and took a few refreshing swallows.

Sarah sat her water down on the table then put her hands together and interlocked her fingers. She took a deep breath then looked at both of them and began to speak.

"Before we start I just want to say this. In order for any consultation to work you have to truthful with yourselves, and I for me to properly help you. You have to have an open mind, and be adequate and fair with your judgment and how you look at your mate. You can't be sexist or one sided, you have to respect your mates perception of things as well as yours. You two are very beautiful and have a lot to offer each other and I'm here to help make this relationship work. Now...I want you to respectfully express yourselves, and my ears are open to hear what you have to say." Sarah expressed, building a sense of balance as the foundation of their conversation.

Cedric and Cynthia glanced at each other to see who would speak first.

"Go ahead." Cedric nodded.

"No, you go." Cynthia replied.

"Well, I love Cynthia very much, and I want our relationship to work. I feel that we get along for the most part, but when we have an issue it seems to over shadow and kill the relationship, and I feel that's because our communication is terrible. We never thoroughly talk about our problems." Cedric expressed.

"That's not true, you just want to talk when you want to talk. Everybody don't want talk right away." Cynthia retorted with a slight attitude.

"See what I'm saying? We can't even have a peaceful consultation without her getting an attitude." Cedric pointed out.

"Because you lying." Cynthia replied.

"Okay wait. Cynthia, do you feel that you guys communicate properly about your issues?" Sarah asked.

"....I feel that we communicate okay sometimes. He just wants things his way and force me to talk when I don't want to. Sometimes I don't want to talk right then." Cynthia answered, glancing over at Cedric.

"And because of that right there" Cedric said just before he was respectfully stopped.

"Hold on Cedric, you will have your turn. I need to understand where she's coming from. Now...Cynthia, why is that you choose to wait before talking about your problems?" Sarah asked.

"Because I be mad at the time, and he ain't gone like the way I talk to him at that time." Cynthia expressed.

"Okay well, I respect that. Now...Cedric, do you have a problem with her having a little bit of space before you guys talk about your problems?" Sarah asked.

"Most of the time Yes, and let me tell you why. First of all if you love me then you shouldn't hate me that bad to the point that you can't talk to me especially if I'm your significant other. Two, every time she walk away or leave out to get her space she get on the phone and talk to her friends about us and express her anger to them and then they tell her something stupid or unfair about me and then she come back talking that heartless stuff to me. And if you can talk to someone that person should be me in the first place because I'm the one you have the issue with." Cedric replied.

"Now, do you know that she goes out and talk to others about you guys relationship or are you just assuming that?" Sarah asked.

"Thank You!!" Cynthia concurred.

"Yes, because it's been times that I'll call a little bit after she leaves and she'll tell me she'll call me back because she's on the phone with one of her girlfriends, and they will put that B.S in her ear and then when I do finally talk to her she'll come home talking a bunch of nonsense to me that had nothing to do with our issue. Or she come back to me comparing our relationship to her girlfriends relationship or her past relationships which I have a big problem with, and that's why I like to iron our stuff out right away to avoid all that stupid drama." Cedric expressed eloquently.

"First of all, I don't come at you on no BS somebody else tells me, I'm my own grown woman. I don't need anyone else's guidance on how to do my relationship." Cynthia said, looking at him with daggering eyes.

"Whatever." Cedric retorted carelessly.

"Whatever, you." Cynthia replied with an attitude and flared nostrils.

"Okay, I want to say something and I need both of Y'all to listen. What I see is a failure to communicate, and the way that you're going about it just doesn't work because you don't respect each other's methods. You want it your way, and he wants it his way and neither one of you are willing to give in. In a relationship you have to give in order to get. You can't always take, take, take, and never give because you drain your mate to the point that they have nothing else to give. I think you Cynthia, need to stop walking away so much and address your problems, and you Cedric, you should allow her to calm herself so that she can come to you in a more peaceful state of mind." Sarah stated.

"Yeah, that's the thing she don't come back peaceful, she come back irrationally lashing out at me ready to break up, after she done went out and had somebody all up in her ear." Cedric said, a bit peeved with the conversation.

"See there you go again insinuating and don't know what you're talking about." Cynthia countered.

"Oh yeah, is that why when I called you the other day you didn't answer the phone for me, but when you pulled up to the house not expecting me to be there you was all giggling on the phone with somebody and then you hurried up and got off the phone and started acting real dry with me. And I will admit I am insinuating that she's been talking to another dude, especially after finding a condom in the car." Cedric revealed.

Cynthia's guilt caused her to pause for a second before she countered.

"I told you that it wasn't mines." Cynthia said as her heart thumped a little harder.

"Now hold on before we get to going there because now you playing with fire. I'm not trying to be the devil's advocate but sometimes unfortunate things can happen like that and it doesn't necessarily have to be hers. Now on the other hand I hope that you're not out here cheating on your mate." Sarah spoke, looking towards Cynthia with a raised eyebrow.

"I'm not." Cynthia replied, lying with a slightly guilt written face.

"Cheating is dangerous, and brings about a world of regret after the little so-called moment of pleasure. People get hurt, killed, not to mention all the different kinds of diseases that are out there, herpes, AIDS, syphilis, you name it. And if I'm correct one out of every four people have AIDS...that means one out of four people are walking around you are sentenced to death and will share their sentence with you in a heartbeat. Now we've been talking about a lot of negative stuff, and I want to talk about the good things that brought you guys together in the first place. I know you guys ultimately want this to work because you wouldn't have agreed to call upon me. So before we go forward with the more beautiful side of this conversation I want you two to get up and give each other a hug." Sarah recommended.

Cedric and Cynthia looked at each other and then got up. They wrapped their arms around each other very meaningfully. Love and guilt was convicting Cynthia as her eyes conceived tears of regret. She really loved Cedric and realized she made a poor decision when she got Damon's number which led to her having sex with him. At that moment she made it up in her mind that she was going to end her secret affair with him and do right by Cedric. Communication, respect, honesty, and trust are four of the keys elements that give birth to a relationship that stands the test of time.

15

When God Speaks... Take Heed

Later that evening Cognac's son, Eric was sitting on the floor in his bedroom playing Halo 4 online on his XBOX 360. He had his head set on and was intensely talking trash back and forth with his opponents. His body twitched and jerked as his thumbs rapidly pressed the buttons, trying to kick some butt online. Cognac was calling Eric's name from the other room but he never responded so she came to his room and stood at the doorway.

"Eric! You don't hear me calling you? Eric?" Cognac asked.

Eric was so into the game that he didn't even realize his mother was calling him.

Cognac walked in front of the TV and then got Eric's attention.

"Ma, what you doing? You're about to get me out!" Eric said as he leaned to the side, trying to see around his mother.

Cognac playfully kneeled down and kissed him on the forehead all while she was making him get out on the game.

"Momma you done made me get out." Eric complained to his Mom.

"That's okay, you need to come and eat anyway." Cognac said as she reached back and turned the power off on the XBOX console and got up.

"Right now, Ma?" Eric asked.

"Yes, now. You don't want to be eating too late, that's not healthy for you. Now go wash your hands and eat that good food Momma done cooked for you." Cognac replied.

"Alright." Eric replied very dry as he got up and headed for the bathroom.

"Don't sound like that, Eric. You better be happy you've got a mother who actually knows how to use a stove and cook you a good meal.

Cognac smiled as she watched her son go to the bathroom to wash his hands. She walked into her livingroom and sat down on her couch. After feeling a slight sharp pain in her stomach she leaned to the side with her head on the pillow, and curled in a fetal position. She did her best not to cry, but was unsuccessful as tears slowly trickled down the side of her face. After a few moments of tearful emotions her cell phone rang. She reached over her head and fiddled around on the table till she felt her phone and grabbed it. She looked at the caller I.D. and saw that it was her Aunt Valerie who claimed guardianship of her when she was younger her after her mother had died.

"Hey Auntie." Cognac said in her withered sounding voice.

"Hey sweetie. How's my baby doing?" Aunt Val asked?

"I'm hanging in there." Cognac uttered.

"Uh oh, you don't sound too good. What's wrong?" Aunt Valerie asked in a subtle, sincere voice.

Cognac sighed with a tear filled face resting on her dampened pillow. She sniffled and then spoke.

"I went to the doctor today because I was feeling pain in my stomach..." Cognac said and paused.

"Okay, and what did the doctor say?"

"...I miscarried." Cognac regretfully uttered.

"I'm so sorry, sweetie. I wish I was there just so I could rub your back like I used to do when you were just a little girl."

A pleasant smile brightened Cognac's lamented face.

"I wish you were here to, Auntie."

"...Well, who's to say that I couldn't be? I could have Regina bring me over there to see my baby."

"That would be nice, Auntie. You've always taken care of me." Cognac said.

"And I always will, sweetie. See you in a little while. I love you."

"I love you too."

"Bye, bye."

"Bye." Cognac said as she hung up her phone with a slight smile.

After a pleasant conversation with her Aunt Val, Cognac eased up and walked into the kitchen to check on Eric. She stopped in her tracks, shook her head and smiled as she looked at him leaned over on the table sleep next to his empty plate of food. She walked over to him and gently rubbed his back. She leaned over and kissed him on the forehead then woke him up so he could go wash up, and get in bed. She took his dishes off of the table and placed them in the sink, ran some dish water, and washed them. Afterwards she wiped down the counter, the table, and the stove. By that time she had heard a car door shut outside and figured that it was Regina, and Aunt Val. She pulled back the curtain to the side window, and looked out. She went and opened the front door, and saw Regina helping Aunt Val get out of the car so she went to help.

"Hey Aunt Val, what happened to your leg?" Cognac asked as she got on the other side of Val, looped her arm around her arm to help her up the stairs.

"Ooohh I'll be okay. These old legs wanna give out on me sometimes but I'll walk on water with cement slippers on to come take care of my baby." Aunt Val said as she closed her eyes and smiled as Cognac kissed her on the cheek.

Regina opened the door, and Val was fine from there as she ease inside the house.

"Hey, I'm sorry, boo." Regina said, referring to the miscarriage and hugged her.

"Thank you." Cognac replied as she tried not to cry.

"I'm going to just sit on down over here on this couch, and want you to come sit right here next to me like you did when you was a little girl." Aunt Val said as she eased down at the end of the couch.

Cognac walked over and sat next to Aunt Val and laid her head on her shoulder. Cognac's eyes watered as she sniffled, trying her best to hold back the tears, but the love she was feeling at the time induced them. Regina sat behind Cognac and placed her hand on her back, and rubbed her gently to comfort her. Aunt Val's words have always been like a touch of paradise, absolutely comforting, and a dose of reality.

"What God has for you, no one or no thing can ever take it away from you. He foresees all and will not place anything on you that you cannot handle. Gold has to be burned by fire in order to purify it. Likewise with the adversities you face they are nothing more than blazing fire burning off your impurities, making you better, just like pure gold. And remember, no weapon formed against you shall prosper for God's Angels will protect you. Now let us stand, and join hands." Aunt Val said very moving.

With very moving words they stood and joined hands. They closed their eyes and bowed their heads.

"Let us pray." Aunt Val said deeply as she spoke a powerful and much needed prayer.

16

Angels

Cognac sat cozy on her couch, leaning on the left arm rest reading a novel. It felt good to have Aunt Val come over and make her feel a lot better with her beautiful and motivating words. She had been going through much hell and unnecessary stress over the past week and was tired of all of it. Cognac thought to call Regina's cell phone and thank her and Aunt Val for stopping by. She picked up her cell phone off of the night stand and dialed Regina's phone. She was slightly caught off guard when she heard the ringing of Regina's phone which was left on her cocktail table. She then dialed Regina's house phone, and left a message for her that she had left her phone. Cognac grew a little concerned when she heard the neighbor's dogs violently barking from the back of the house so. She sat her book down, got up and calmly went to go investigate. On the way down the hall she peeped in Eric's room and saw that he was sleep. She proceeded down the hall to the den and peeked through the horizontal blinds to see if she saw anything strange. She looked left, she looked right, and saw nothing out of order. She turned around and screamed as her heart beat fluttered seriously. Behold...there he stood...black leather gloves on his hands, while the right hand clutched a stainless steel thirty-eight revolver... the cold lost stare in his eyes made him appear a bit possessed... With his left index finger vertically up to his lips, he told her to shhhh and don't say a word or die.

"Stop being loud, I'm sure you don't want lil Eric being a part of this." Marcello said with an intimidating stare in his eyes.

"What are you doing here, and how did you get in here?!" Cognac asked, breathing heavily, and a face filled with shock.

"What do you mean? I'm here visiting my baby Momma. How did I get in here? The same way I've always got in here...A key. You never changed the locks, Cognac." Marcello said as he twirled the key to the house on a key ring wrapped around his index finger.

"What do you want from me?" Cognac asked.

"Justice." Marcello uttered.

"What are you talking about, Marcello?" Cognac asked with tearful eyes.

"I'm talking about...Justice, your understanding. I tried talking to you and explaining it and you just wouldn't listen. You rather talk all hard, and diss me with your cold hearted responses. You never put forth the effort to understand, and consider my side of the story. You didn't even take the time to think that maybe you had something to do with me having sex with your friend." Marcello replied.

"You committed the injustice, not me. How did I have anything to do with you fucking my friend in my house?" Cognac asked.

"Come on Coney, you're a lot smarter than that, sweetie. People like you kill me always wanting to crucify someone but never want to crucify thy self. You're the one who always invited your friend over while we smoked and got high. You're the one who kissed, touched, and grabbed all over me right in front of her, enticing her, tempting her, seducing her. She even made a comment about joining us while watching you kiss and grope on me. You were like a fucking porno star in action, making anybody that's watching it want a piece of it."

"So you're saying it's my fault?"

"I'M SAYING YOU WERE THE TEMPTRESS THAT BROUGHT THIS ON. The same way Eve brought the forbidden fruit to Adam is the same way you brought the forbidden fruit to me. And now you want to stand here and act blameless and perfect." Marcello uttered with a wicked look on his face.

"Momma..." Eric called out from the other room.

Cognac feared for her son's life when she heard his feet sweeping across the floor. She yelled for him to go back to bed, but by that time he was standing in the doorway rubbing his eyes.

"I couldn't sleep Momma. Oh hey Marcello." Eric said with a beautiful smile as he walked over to Marcello, and hugged him.

Marcello carefully eased his hand with the gun in it behind his back, and hugged him.

"Wsup lil fella?" Marcello asked kindly as he sinisterly glanced over at Cognac.

"Eric, go get back in bed." Cognac said.

"Mom, can Marcello play the video game with me?" Eric said, wanting to kick it Marcello for a moment.

"NO, NOW GET OVER HERE TO ME!" Cognac commanded.

With a sad face Eric slowly eased over to Cognac. She immediately grabbed Eric's hand and pulled him behind her and looked at Marcello with worry, and hate written on her face.

"Why are you looking so mean?" Marcello asked as he walked up on them very slowly.

"Don't do this." Cognac pleaded with a tear filled tightened face.

"And oh yeah, as far as that married bullshit. If I was married there's no way I would've able to be with you every single day with no problem, no harassing phone calls, being out in public and not trying to be seen. We never went through that bullshit, so maybe if you would've used your brain instead of your got damn emotions then maybe it would've dawned on you that perhaps I'm not actually married. That piece of paper don't mean shit."

"Then why did you tell me not to have the baby?" Cognac asked.

"Because until the divorce was finalized she could have used it against me in court. Are divorce just hadn't got finalized yet, but did that mean I was supposed to be fucking lonely or couldn't meet someone and move on?" Marcello asked.

"Marcello, don't do this, please?" Cognac asked.

"I tried to thoroughly explain to you what was going on but you refused to accept reality. And now your selfish decisions have become a problem that I am unable to live with." Marcello said as he slowly stepped closer to them.

She told Eric to close his eyes tight and keep them shut. Cognac's pulse rushed as she closed her eyes and tightened her lips together. With long heavy breaths she lowered her head as she recalled the precious words of her Aunt.

"No weapon formed against me shall prosper." Cognac uttered in a seriously low voice.

"Oh yeah, well...all that scripture stuff ain't bout to save you now." Marcello replied in a low, wicked voice.

Marcello raised the pistol, and was violently cracked over the side of the head with a black cast iron skillet cutting him just below the right eye. Marcello helplessly fell to the floor, dropping the gun as Regina stood ominously over him still holding the skillet. Cognac told Eric to go call the police and tell them someone came into their house and tried to attack him and his mother. Cognac picked up the gun, and then stood over him pointing the gun at his face.

"He got a lot of damn nerve coming up in my house and threatening me, and endangering the life of my son! After all the bullshit he put me through!...I was a faithful, good woman to him, and this is how I'm rewarded? I WILL NEVER GET PLAYED BY ANOTHER MAN AGAIN!! Ima be the one doing the playing." Cognac said as she cocked the pistol.

Regina saw that Cognac was extremely

enraged, and when add a gun into the equation the outcome can be detrimental.

"He ain't even worth it, Coney. He ain't even worth it. Let the police come get this scum." Regina said to calm Cognac.

17

Succulent Surprise

Antonio cruised westward up Outer Drive RD coming from Sherwood Forest, a beautiful and well kept community that highlights Detroit Michigan. A bouquet of roses lie in the passenger seat that he had picked up from the Sherwood Floral Gift Shop. Seven thin pink ribbons tied to seven pink, and white balloons with red lettering and designs on them were strapped around the bouquet to keep them in place. He made a left onto Pennington St, and pulled up in front of the driveway of the seventh house on the right. He put the car in park then reached inside of his inner coat pocket and pulled out a small thinking of you card. He grabbed a pen then wrote "Just to make you smile." And just below that he signed "Sincerely Antonio". He stuck the card in between the plastic teeth of the pitch fork stuck inside the flowers. He got out of his car and carefully walked up to her car that was parked in her driveway. He had only been by there one time before and he hoped that he had the right house. The license plate on her car read PEACHES so he knew that he had the right house. He walked to the front of the car and double wrapped the balloons around the windshield blade of her car, and placed the roses on top so they wouldn't blow around so much and get loose. He turned and walked away headed to his car so he could pull up the street and call peaches and tell her to look at her car so she could find her surprise.

"That's how you do it? You just surprise a lady with some beautiful flowers, and balloons, and then just leave like that?" Peaches asked, leaning out the side door.

Antonio looked back and said "You weren't supposed to see that. It was supposed to be a surprise."

"And it was. I just happened to walk into the kitchen and see you through the window. I was making some hot tea. Would you like some before you go? I know you're cold by now." Peaches asked.

"Yeah...I can use a little something to heat me up." Antonio said with sly smirk on his face.

"I'm talking about Tea heating you up, not the P." Peaches said as she stepped outside and unraveled the balloons, and grabbed the flowers off of the windshield.

She stepped inside then held the door open and invited him in. Her attraction to him caused her to look at him up and down in a delectable way as he walked past her while she closed the door. She had him take off his coat and hang it on the back of the kitchen chair. She put the flowers to her nose, closed her eyes and sniffed.

"I looove the smell of flowers, and these smell so good. And I love the balloons too. Thank you." Peaches said with a smile as she let the balloons float to the ceiling off in the corner so that they would be out of the way, and then gave Antonio a hug.

"You welcome, sweetie. It ain't nothing like beautiful flowers that compliment a beautiful Goddess." Antonio said.

Peaches enjoyed his arms being wrapped around her frame. The smell of his Roca Wear cologne caused her vaginal juices to condensate making her panties moist. Antonio loved the fresh clean smell of her getting out of the shower, and the light scent of body spray she put on.

"Okayyyyyyyy let me um, go, I need to stay focused." Peaches said as she tried to control her urges and imagination of having the most reckless sex you could ever experience.

If he would've held her any longer she knew he would've been boning her ass right there on the kitchen counter. She turned around and walked to the sink then reached into the cabinet just below and pulled out an empty vase. She turned on the water then ran some into the vase and then placed the flowers inside. She sat the flowers down on the counter then grabbed the cabinet door and opened it. Standing on her tip toes she reached up to the second shelf but couldn't quite get a good grip on the box of tea. Antonio was admiring the view and how her pink PHAT FARM Baby T shirt gave emphasis to her sexy torso, and her pink stretch pants

Men-Tal

made her fat perfectly rounded ass look so tasty.

"Let me get that for you?" Antonio said as he walked over to grab the tea.

Peaches backed up, and almost in slow motion she admired every movement of his body. She loved the way his triceps flexed as he reached up, and nicely trimmed stomach. The bulge in his pants caused her mouth to salivate. She quickly gathered herself after he pulled the tea down off of the shelf. Even though she liked him she didn't want to appear vulnerable by allowing him to know how much she liked him. She had been scarred by past relationships so much that she would use her standoffishness as a defensive mechanism to protect her heart; although this type of defensive mechanism can cause you to lose out on something good that God has sent to you as well. He handed her the tea and then leaned back up against the adjacent counter while she prepared the tea. She turned the stove eye off once the water had come to a boil. She grabbed two cups from out of the cabinet and sat them on the counter then made the tea. She turned around and handed him his tea.

"Be careful now, it's hot." Peaches said.

"I'm pretty sure you'll take care of me. I remember when you told me that nursing was another love of yours." Antonio said.

"Yeah, I'll take care of you alright." Peaches said sarcastically yet playful.

"Trust me, I would LOOOOOVE for nurse Peaches to take care of me. I'll keep getting ill just so I could see you in that sexy uniform." Antonio said as he sipped his tea.

He immediately flinched, pretending that he had burned the shit out of his mouth.

"You okay?" Peaches asked very concerned as she grabbed a piece of ice from out of one of the ice trays in the freezer.

She walked up to him and placed the piece of ice on his lip and held it there.

"I told you to be careful, Antonio. Is this where it burns at?" Peaches asked, and Antonio nodded yes.

Their chemistry was extremely compelling. The long time physical attraction mixed with mental stimulation, and compassion made each touch feel like paradise. Her lips looked honey sweet sticky, and soft. She could feel it inside that they were about to take it there. He slowly eased closer to her and kissed her jaw just next to her lips. The urge was too much for her to fight as they slowly engaged in a kiss on the lips which turned into deep, passionate bottom lip nibbling kiss. She gently wrapped her arms around the back of his neck and with her right hand she stroked the crown of his head. His strong hands smoothly moved down her back, and fingers traced her protruding ass. Breathing accelerated as the kiss grew a little bit more serious...a little bit more seductive, I want you in the most nastiest way type of kiss. She took his shirt off then dropped it on the floor and started kissing and nibbling his chest. He leaned forward and softly French kissed her neck, her weak spot. She took her left hand and began rubbing on his rock hard dick. Still engaged in the most passionate kiss she took both hands and unzipped his pants. She stuck her hand inside and gave him a pleasurable massage. Slowly she kissed his chest, his stomach, then twirled her tongue in his navel. She unbuttoned his pants and without hesitation she allowed herself to taste what her mouth had been salivating for. He closed his eyes, and moaned as he tilted his head back in ecstasy. She pulled his pants off and gave him an intense tongue massage from the scrotum to the head. Sucking, slurping, and stroking, she gave him the paradise head every man dreams of. He had her get up and started kissing her as he slipped her stretch pants down, and off. He cuffed her ass with both hands and sat her top of the counter. He slid her panties off and just flung them somewhere behind them, and then parted her legs with her toes extended in opposite directions. The sweet scent of her pheromones and the taste of her vaginal juice seduced him to passionately lick and suck her pussy like the sweetest and most delicious exotic fruit on the face of the earth. She moaned and sighed as her fingers and toes stiffened. Her head rolled back as she cuffed the back of his head, burying his face deeper causing her breathing and pulse to rush. With his goatee saturated with her secretions he stood up fully erect and stuck his dick inside of her. She gasped in pleasurable ecstasy the deeper he entered. He gripped her hips and stroked her harder, and made her explode as she tightly griped the edge of the counter. Antonio had her wrap her arms around his neck and told her to hold on. He placed his arms under her legs and palmed her ass as he lifted her off of the counter and walked her into the livingroom with his dick still throbbing inside of her. The sensation made Peaches feel like she could cum a thousand times just from the non-stop dick action. He sat down on the couch with her mounted on top of him and immediately she straddled him like she was riding a mustang. After while it was only right that he place an ass like that in a doggy-style position. He had her get up and calmly bent her over on the couch. She parted her legs and arched her back as she provided a crazy lustful X-Rated visual from a man's most wanton dreams. He inserted himself deeply and stroked, and stroked deeper, harder, breaking her off the way she loves it. She gripped the top of the backrest of the couch tightly, and looked back at him as she threw that ass back. He could no longer hold back so he pulled out and stroked his shaft till he came all over her ass. Breathing heavily Antonio sat down on the couch and calmly relaxed himself after some intensified, unexpected beautiful sex. Peaches walked to the bathroom, looked in the mirror and exhaled with a slight look of disappointment on her face. She had been this route before feeling vulnerable and exposed. Making love to this man with feelings attached was in violation of her personal rules that are to protect her heart. Her emotions started getting the best of her and she regretted making love to him period. She turned the water on in the face bowl then bent down, scooping water into her hands and rinsed her face. She grabbed a clean wash cloth from the cabinet and wiped her face dry. She then lathered the wash cloth with some soap and water and briefly washed up. She grabbed the matching towel, dried off and then wrapped it around her body.

"You look so damn beautiful, and making love to you felt so right." Antonio said as he stopped at the doorway admiring her with a pleasant smile on his face.

Peaches remained silent for a couple of seconds as she glanced over at him and looked in the mirror, reminding herself to stay strong. She grabbed another wash cloth and a towel from the cabinet and handed it to him.

"Just leave them on the edge of the tub when you done, I'll get em." Peaches said as she walked past him and headed to the livingroom.

Antonio was confused as of why she appeared a bit dry and disappointed. He thought to himself as he washed up that she just couldn't have been faking the feeling after a performance like that. He dried himself off after he finished and walked up front, picked up his boxers and put them on. He put on his pants and walked into the livingroom. He pulled his shirt on over his head and noticed she hadn't even acknowledged that he had even walked into the livingroom as she just sat there with her legs crossed reading a Jet magazine. He knew that something was disturbing her after she flipped the script from enjoying some explosive, passionate sex to regretting that he was even in her presence. And being that he knew he hadn't disrespected her or convinced her into doing anything that she wasn't willing to do herself then he could only figure it to be one thing...she was scared of being hurt.

"Based off of your abrupt actions I take it that you're scared." Antonio said.

"I don't know what makes you say that, I'm straight." Peaches said as she nonchalantly continued reading her magazine with her legs crossed and foot dangling.

"Okay then, what did I do to deserve the standoffish attitude?" Antonio asked, feeling as if he wasn't wanted around at the time.

"I'm just not about to get played like the rest of the girls, and fall for the little mesmerizing facade you're putting up for now. Y'all dudes come with the mind games and get all up in a woman's head to get some ass, and I must admit you got me good, nobody ever came at me like that before. Tying flowers and balloons to the windshield blade of my car, and your sweet and kind words got me open. You've conquered your goal and got the cookies, bravo." Peaches said as she sarcastically clapped her hands slowly.

"Oh so you're one of them type of women? Think God only made good women and no good men? You're one of them women who was attracted to bad men and got hurt, and now you wanna color every good man bad based off of a poor selection of men in your past."

"Who do you think you are? Some type of mind reader now?" Peaches asked, taking offense to what he was saying although it was true.

"I'm someone telling you the truth about yourself. If I was one of these dudes treating you like shit you probably would fabricate reasons to look at me as a good man just to validate your thirst for scum dudes.

"At least I know what I'm getting into ahead of time. I've dealt with those type of dudes before so I know what to expect. Maybe if my father was at home when I was growing up then perhaps I would see things differently. But because I didn't have that luxury I have to protect my heart even if it means dating scum dudes or whatever you want to call them." Peaches replied.

"I hear you. And as profound as you may sound I must admit that is some of the dumbest shit I've ever heard. You don't keep taking poison just because you've learned something about it, and the harm that it does to you. And you can't just blame the lack of what you know on the absence of your father because what does that say about the presence of your mother? Just because one parent isn't around doesn't mean the other parent isn't supposed to teach. I stayed with my father all of my life, and only saw my mother twice, but my father didn't let that stop him from teaching me what a good woman is like. But whatever, when you decide you can appreciate a good man then you call me, you got my number." Antonio said as he turned and headed for the door.

Peaches was momentarily speechless as she watched him head out the side door and calmly shut it behind him. She knew that he was right about what he was saying, and she felt someone regretful about how she treated him. She swiftly walked to the door, opening it up, and leaned out.

"Wait." Peaches said, stopping him in his tracks.

He turned back around and slowly walked up to her. She took a deep breath and exhaled with a bit of sincerity in her eyes.

"I apologize for the way I acted, I didn't mean to offend you or hurt your feelings in anyway. Thank you for the flowers and balloons, that was very sweet of you."

Peaches confessed as she leaned forward and hugged him.

"No problem."

"I...I just need time to heal...I just haven't figured how yet." Peaches sincerely added.

"That's wsup, but just know that healing doesn't just come from the elapse of time, but by forgiveness and letting go of your past. You can't build a new house on an old raggedy foundation. Be blessed." Antonio said as he turned and headed for his car.

Peaches slowly shut the door then pulled back the curtain, and watched him pull off down the street. Once you learn right from wrong your bad choices are the responsibility of no one else other than yourself.

18

Love and Roulette

9:37pm **New Years Eve, and** the low mellow sound of soulful slow jams serenaded the atmosphere. The chandelier lights were dimmed perfectly and dawned up Cynthia as she sat at the candle lit dining room table looking gorgeous. She enjoyed the song of Luther Vandross as she patiently awaited her surprise dinner. The sound of a cork popped then Cedric walked into the dining room and approached the table with two champagne glasses and a bottle of Moet. He poured a glass about three quarters of the way and sat it in front of her. He poured another glass and sat it in front of where he was going to be sitting then sat the bottle down on a coaster in the middle of the table. He walked back into the kitchen and returned with two designer plates of delicious looking food, grilled chicken, brown rice, and steamed long stemmed green beans made to perfection. He sat both plates on the table and took a seat adjacent to where she was sitting.

"Wow, the food looks delicious." Cynthia said, admiring the creativity.

"Thank you. I just wanted this night to be beautiful and show the woman I love just how special she is to me." Cedric replied.

"Mmmmm this food is delicious." Cynthia said as she placed a fork full in her mouth.

"Thank you, I'm glad you liked it." Cedric said.

"I think you trying to get me fat, cooking me all this good food like this." Cynthia said as she smirked at him with her lips twisted.

"No not all of you, just the booty, baby." Cedric replied, leaning to the side glimpsing at her ass.

"Whatever, all this is about to be gone. You ain't gone be able to tell me nothing this summer." Cynthia replied, rubbing on her thigh and ass.

"Why do women always talk about losing the very part of their bodies that drives their man wild the most? I just don't get that."

"I ain't trying to lose all of it, just some. Besides I've always had a booty, that ain't gone change. I just want to get down to like a size seven."

"Size seven? You trying to get all scrawny like them sick looking chicks off of them Top Model shows."

"I just don't like looking fat."

"Why do you keep saying that you are fat? You're nowhere near fat."

"According to studies on women's height and weight I'm twenty pounds overweight for my height."

"Yeah but that study isn't accurate for all women. For instance, black women carry their weight beautifully. How much you weigh?"

"I'm not telling you." Cynthia said with her face frowned up.

"What are you hiding your weight from me for? I love the way you look."

"I weigh one-fifty three

Cedric loved Cynthia sincerely and did everything in his power to make her happy like a good man should. Although the mood was set perfectly with the dinner, champagne and music he knew inside that her mind was somewhere else. Cedric brought up conversation about their past elaborating about how he adored her ever since they briefly dated in high school. They reminisced about how they broke up once she discovered her family was moving to Atlanta and of course she had no choice but to leave as well. They figured it must've been heaven sent after running into each other in their late twenties at a local bar with some of their friends and reunited. The conversation brought forth beautiful feelings and smiles as they ate and got tipsy off of Moet. Her cell phone rang in her holster on her hip, and she just ignored it, afraid that it might be Damon. Cedric kept his composer but silently paid attention to see if she would answer or not. She elaborated on the subject that they were talking about to take his mind off of the fact that she didn't want to answer her phone. Two minutes later her phone rang again and she raised it half way out of the case and glanced at it. Her heart thumped a little bit faster when she saw Damon's name on the screen and put it back in the case. Cedric couldn't help but become suspicious.

"So are you just going to keep ignoring your phone like you got something to hide?" Cedric asked.

"I'll get to it later. I don't want any interruptions, I just want to enjoy this beautiful meal that you made me." Cynthia replied.

"Cynthia, Ima ask you one time. Have you been cheating on me?"

"N, no, I, I told you I haven't been cheating. We're supposed to be trusting each other like we said we would do at the consultation. You gave your word and said that you wouldn't falsely accuse me." Cynthia replied.

"Then let me see your phone?"

"Then what was the use of us getting the consultation if you're going to continue falsely accusing me every time my phone rings, or I leave out the door?" Cynthia asked.

Cedric sat there silently thinking to himself about everything they talked about during the consultation. He wanted to trust her but part of him just didn't. He looked down at the table thinking, repeatedly tapping it with his fingers. He looked up, straight into her eyes.

"Okay...if I'm wrong I apologize...but let me say this...if I find out you're cheating, it's not going to be pretty. I'm about to go lay down for a moment...I hope you enjoyed dinner." Cedric said as he stood up and walked out the room.

"Are we still gonna go to the New Years Eve Ball tonight?" Cynthia asked, and never got a reply.

The candle light reflected from Cynthia's face as she sat there thinking about how she had to end her affair with Damon immediately. She realized Cedric was a good man and that she was going to lose him messing around with some dude who didn't mean anything to her. She figured she'd wait a moment and let Cedric cool off and then go in the room with him and please him like a King is supposed to be pleased. A tear trickled from her dazed eyes as she sat there staring out the livingroom window at the flurries of snow coming down. Truth always comes to the light.

19

New Years Eve Toast

10pm **Cognac, Benita, Peaches** were gathered over Regina's house in her basement getting themselves ready for the Chocolate and Cream New Years Ball. Hip Hop, and R&B was playing through the speakers, making the vibe just right as they listened to their favorite local radio station. Along one of the basement walls were five, six foot mirrors surrounded by sphere shaped vanity lights. The ladies were all looking succulent and tantalizing in their dresses, and stilettos. Hair-doo's, whipped, feather wraps, and quick weaves were fly. The tip of the lip gloss traced Peaches thick sexy lips giving her that sticky, shinny affect that every man would love to taste. She looked herself up and down then blew a kiss to herself. Cognac stood to the side fixing her dress, admiring the way it beautifully accentuated her ass righteously. Benita took her lip liner and traced the edge of her eyelid and put a sharp point at the outer end. Regina had a nice little buzz going on and was ready to enjoy the night. Regina let everyone know that it was time for a refill and took the bottle around and poured more champagne for everyone.

"I'd like to propose a toast." Regina said, holding up her glass.

"That's what I'm talking about." Peaches replied, holding her glass up, feeling good and shaking her hips to the music.

Benita, and Cognac joined in holding their glasses up ready to make a grand toast.

"First I would like to say that it is a blessing to be standing here with my cousin and both of my girls who are closer to me than some of my own family. I am so glad to have you Goddesses by my side, and having my back. Our friendship has been genuine since day one and has never changed. And I want toast to true friendship." Regina said.

"I want to toast to a love, peace, and prosperity filled New Year." Peaches added.

"I'm totally feeling what Regina was saying and I just want to add that it feels good to have some true sistas around me that I can call on if I ever need to. It ain't all that jealousy and hate, we are what sistas are supposed to be to each other, honorable and true." Benita added.

Regina, Cognac and Peaches agreed.

"Cognac?" Regina asked as they all looked at Cognac.

Cognac looked at them as if she were surprised that it was her turn to say something.

"Oh, well um I just want to toast to being single and saying fuck love." Cognac said.

"Aw come on Coney don't be like that. That was just one clown who pissed you off. Come on we're speaking positivity into our new year." Regina said.

"Alright well, I want to toast to being a stronger, wiser, and more selective woman in this New Year. Oh, and Essential Beauty Salon CONTINUING to be the number one salon and kicking ass and doing the best hair-do's period, hands down." Cognac said profoundly.

"Now I'm with that." Peaches concurred.

"That's so wsup. Well ladies lets go have fun, have some drinks, meet some real men that are actually doing something positive in their lives and not dope selling. So, Ladies, Diva's, Goddesses let's make our wishes come true...Cheers." Regina proposed as they prepared to go get live at the New Years Eve Ball.

...DAYUM

20

Chocolate and Cream Ball

The sound of stilettos click clacked across the concrete as Regina, Cognac, Peaches, and Benita approached the prestigious night club. Gorgeous statues of Lions, Elephants, and other exotic animals aligned the walk way that led up to the door. Above the door read "Millennium Night's." A line of people waiting to get in was formed just outside the door so the ladies got in line as well.

"Damn, look at this long ass line. We bout to be freezing." Peaches said as her teeth started to chatter.

"We'll be alright, the line moving pretty quick so just be cool. Oops I mean um, think about something warm like a hot beach in Miami." Benita replied.

"You think about a hot beach in Miami. I'm thinking about walking back to the car and waiting until Y'all get up to the door and then come get back in line." Peaches responded, holding her shivering body and lips quivering.

"By time you do all that we'll be walking inside the place. The line does look like its moving pretty good." Regina said, adding a positive outlook to the moment.

Just ahead of them were a few females waiting in line with no coats on. Benita noticed it and figured she could use that to make Peaches feel a tiny bit better by mixing facts with a little humor.

"That is so cheap and stupid." Benita blurted out to her girls while shamefully shaking her head.

"What?" Cognac asked.

"It's twenty damn degrees outside and you're going to leave your coat in the car just so you can save three funky ass dollars on a coat check? Hell, I guarantee you a couple of they asses is going to have a cold or fever by tomorrow. And when they do, they are going to be marching their asses to the pharmacy buying medicine that cost twice as much as coat check. I swear I love my sistas but I must say they can do some dumb shit sometimes." Benita expressed.

"Oh I see em, hell nall. I don't know what be on some of these females minds. They be trying to look cute but don't know they be looking desperate and stupid as hell. I ain't about to freeze to look good for no dude, or to save two or three dollars at a coat check. Shiiit I feel warm as hell now." Peaches added.

"Y'all are a mess." Regina replied.

After about eight or nine minutes they were inside checking their coats in. The club was an enormous three stories, and people were partying on each floor. A huge rectangular shaped bar was at the center of the club with people all around it ordering everything from Margarita's to Hennessey. A light bluish huge chandelier cascaded from the lights above creating a chill atmosphere. As they walked further Cognac happened to run into Demarco who had invited her.

"Cognac? What's up, baby?" Demarco asked, extending his hand for a gentle handshake.

"Hey Demarco, how you doing?" Cognac asked as she shook his hand, silently admiring his touch.

"I'm fine, sweetie. How about you? You looking sexy." Demarco said, checking her out, admiring her beauty.

"Well thank you. You look very handsome. Oh, let me introduce you to some of my girls I'm here with. This is Regina, This is Benita, and this is Peaches." Cognac respectfully introduced.

"Nice to meet you beautiful ladies. If Y'all want to sit next to the bar I have a table over there." Demarco suggested.

Cognac looked at her girls and asked "Y'all fine sitting next to the bar?"

Her girls didn't mind so she looked back at Demarco "That's fine.

Demarco showed them to their table.

"What you ladies drink, white or dark?" Demarco asked.

"We doing white tonight." Cognac answered.

"Okay I got Y'all, just give me a sec, and I'll send the waitress over here." Demarco said.

"Okay, thank you." Cognac replied with a smile.

"You welcome, sweetie." Demarco said and walked away.

Cognac and her girls were checking him out as he walked away. It feels good to be the one to get you and your people special treatment.

"Alright Coney, you getting love for you and your girls as soon as we come through the door. That's how you bring in the New Years." Peaches said, grinning and nudging Cognac on the arm.

"It ain't no fun if my girls can't have none." Cognac said playfully as her girls smiled and high fived.

"So when did you meet him?" Regina asked, grinning at Cognac wanting to know the details.

"That's the one I told you gave me the tickets right before crazy ass Marcello pulled up and we got into it.

"That's right, you did say that. Well, I'm glad that crazy sucka gone. You needed a fresh start." Regina replied.

The waitress walked over to the table with a fifth of Patron on ice, a large bottle of cranberry juice just in case someone wanted a chaser, and four glasses. She sat the glasses down, poured their drinks for them, and sat the bottle in the middle of the table.

"You ladies let me know if you need anything else. As for now I hope you ladies are hungry because he ordered a steak and seafood platter that I'll be bringing out to you very shortly." The waitress said.

"Oohh yes, tell him I said thank you." Cognac replied.

"I sure will, and I'll be back with your food shortly." The waitress said then walked away.

"Girl, I'm taking notes from your ass from now on." Benita said.

"Well I'm about to take notes of how fast I can find the bathroom because I have to go." Cognac replied, looking around for a restroom.

"Me too, let's go before the food gets here." Peaches suggested.

Peaches and Cognac got up and walked to the restroom. Their sexy asses were the center of attention, gaining the focus of men and women. Just a couple of tables over was a guy and his woman eating some chicken nachos and having some drinks. His girl noticed Cognac and Peaches walking by. She also noticed that both of them had fat round asses and immediately she looked at her man.

"I know you was looking at them hoes that just walked by." The girlfriend said, referring to Cognac and Peaches.

"What the hell are you talking about?" The boyfriend asked after putting a fork of food in his mouth.

"Don't play with me, you just looked at them hoes right there when you thought I wasn't looking." The girlfriend said with a stank look on her face.

"What fucking hoes are you talking about? I ain't even looked at no damn body. I'm up here trying to eat my damn food." The boyfriend said as he looked behind him to see what she was talking about.

"Oh, you gone turn around and look at them hoes?" The girlfriend asked, irrationally.

"I'm trying to see what the hell you talking about! I hadn't seen neither one of them until you pointed them out." The boyfriend replied.

"Whatever! You can have them hoes if you want. They ain't got shit on me." The girlfriend said as she looked down at her body.

"Why the hell you talk stupid every time you notice a lady with a fat ass and a pretty face? I don't even be looking, and you still trip on me, and you wonder why we never go out! I don't feel like hearing this shit. I need a damn drink. Ah, waiter, I need some more drinks over here! Please?" The boyfriend yelled out.

On the way to the restroom Cognac and Peaches came across a table with a chocolate fountain and an array of square white plates with chocolate covered strawberries and drizzles of chocolate fondue all around it for design. At the opposite end of the table was an ice cream machine surrounded by small round bowls of peanuts, and chocolate sprinkles so you can make your Chocolate and Cream Theme desert just the way you like it. Cognac and Peaches decided they wanted to taste test, and did so. Peaches picked up one of the plates with two chocolate covered strawberries on it and tasted one.

"Mmmmmmm girl these chocolate covered strawberries taste good as hell." Peaches emphasized as she bit one.

"Let me try one?" Cognac asked as she reached for one off of Peaches plate.

"Un uh girl, you better get you own!" Peaches said as she moved her plate.

Cognac picked up a plate and tasted one.

"Damn, these do taste good." Cognac responded.

They finished off their early desert and proceeded to the restroom. Back at the table Regina, and Benita were sipping their drinks, and talking about everything that was going on.

"Oh Cognac got it going on tonight. Ole boy straight up laying it out for her." Benita said.

"Yeah, but it's something about that dude that alarms me, I just can't put a finger on it. It's like I've seen him somewhere before." Regina said as she thought about it.

"Lord, please don't tell me you used to kick it with him before?" Benita asked.

"Nall! Why?" Regina asked, with a crazy look on her face.

"I just don't want no type of confusion to come up so we can keep getting free food and drinks." Benita said being silly.

"Girl bye. He just looks familiar that's all. I ain't trippin on that, I'm ready to get my party on." Regina replied as she sipped her drinks.

By this time Cognac and Peaches came walking out of the restroom. They looked over at the dance floor filled with people doing their thang and said they would be going out there as soon as they finished eating. As they were headed back to their seat a familiar voice caught her attention.

"Hello Ms. Cognac." Keith said.

Cognac looked and it tripped her out that it was the handsome brotha who wrapped his number in that roll of twenty and fifty dollar bills from footlocker.

"Keith, right?" Cognac said with a smile.

"Yup that's me. You killing it in that dress sexy mamma." Keith said, admiring her beauty and curves.

"Boy you know you be running that good game." Cognac replied, loving every bit of what he was saying.

"This ain't no game, I keep everything one hunnet, and I'm just calling it how I see it." Keith replied.

"Mmmmm" Peaches responded only so Cognac heard it.

"Oh Keith this is my girl Peaches, Peaches this is Keith." Cognac introduced.

"Nice to meet you." Keith said, nodding his head.

"Nice to meet you." Peaches replied.

"Look, why don't Y'all come and join me and a couple of my partners over here at the table and have a few drinks or something?" Keith asked.

"Well look we got some food coming that we're about to eat. So how about we catch up with Y'all afterwards, and maybe we can get on the dance floor?" Cognac suggested.

"Sounds like a winner." Keith replied.

"Okay see you around." Cognac said as she and Peaches turned and walked to their table.

Keith was checking out the ass as she walked away. The way it moved was definitely poetry in motion, and the lust and envy in everyone's eyes that looked upon. He had no plans on letting her slip through his hands this time.

Just as Cognac, and Peaches sat down the food was being brought out to the table. The waitress laid a steak and seafood platter down on the table. Four, well done New York strip steaks, four, medium size lobsters with butter sauce and lemon slices on the side, twenty battered shrimp with a side of cocktail sauce, and a basket of seasoned fries. The food looked delectable and the ladies were good and hungry.

"Can I get you ladies anything else?" The waitress asked.

"Four waters, please." Cognac requested.

"No problem, I'll be right back." The waitress replied and walked away.

"Hey, has anybody heard from Cynthia, or Cedric?" Benita asked.

"I haven't. I tried calling both of them earlier but I didn't get an answer. I called Cynthia right before we left out my house and still got the voicemail so I just left a message." Regina answered as she ate a piece of her lobster.

"I tried calling her too. Well at least they can't say we didn't try reaching them." Benita replied, sipping her drink.

"Hey guess who I saw a few days ago." Benita said.

"Who?" Regina asked, sipping her drink.

"Duce sorry ass." Benita answered shaking her head.

"What?! What was he doing?" Regina asked.

"Standing outside in the snow looking pitiful next to his stuff his apartment complex sat out on the curb."

"See, God don't like ugly." Regina said.

"Well he better be glad I didn't see him because I would've drove by and splashed some dirty cold slush off the ground on his ugly ass." Peaches said real mean.

"Damn, Peaches." Cognac replied, laughing.

"I ain't no mean person, but I can't stand for nobody to steal from me." Peaches replied.

For the next ten minutes they talked, and got their eat and drink on like it was no tomorrow. Ain't nothing like some deliciously made food and a good ass drink to get the vibe right. After finishing their food they decided they wanted to go and hit the dance floor. So they got up and left their "reserved" sign on the table and went to get their groove on.

"Hey, ain't that Antonio?" Cognac asked, pointing towards the bar.

"Where?" Peaches asked.

"The Antonio that just started working with us?" Regina asked.

"Yeah that's him." Peaches replied as they approached.

They all stopped to say what up to Antonio who was sitting at the bar with his boy, Dennis. They introduced themselves and got acquain'ted real quickly. Antonio offered to buy them a round of drinks but they requested that he did so after they came off of the dance floor. The song booty call came on so Cognac and her girls hurried up and strolled to the dance floor. Antonio and his boy Dennis sat there admiring the view as they walked away.

"Got damn, all them got fat asses!" Dennis said as he down his 1800 shot.

"I know, dog. Nothing but ass for days." Antonio replied as he downed his 1800 shot and sipped his Carona right behind it.

"Nigga, what if we had all four of they asses , just me and you up in a hotel with all the blunts and drinks we need? Especially your girl Cognac, I'll fuck the dog shit out of her fat ass for real!" Dennis emphasized as he sipped his Bud Light.

"You wouldn't even know what to do if she put all that ass on you, dog." Antonio stated.

"Nigga, is you crazy? I'll beat the brakes off that ass, trust me. I'm just trippin as of why you ain't knocked off that little sexy ass Peaches chick. I seen her giving you the eye contact." Dennis said.

"Who said I didn't?" Antonio asked as he looked out onto the dance floor.

"Nigga, you ain't hit that." Dennis replied, waiving his hand with the whatever look on his face.

Antonio just turned and looked at him with the Ima G face, and Dennis said "My nigga." and gave him some dap.

The dance floor was real live as hell as a bunch of sexy ass women and a few men did the Chicago hustle in unison. Keith and his boys stood off to the side looking at Cognac and her girls get their dance on. Keith was feeling his buzz and loving the way Cognac was moving. She cracked a smile a few times whenever she spun around and got eye contact with him. Just as the song was going off Antonio walked onto the dance floor and got behind Peaches and started dancing. She looked back and saw that it was him and started bouncing that ass all over him. Cognac and everybody else just kept getting their groove on. After that song went off the music slowed down with a nice sexy slow jam. Cognac, Regina, and Benita went back to their table. Antonio and Peaches put their arms around each other and enjoyed the pleasurable moment. The DJ announced that it was a minute left before the New Year. Everyone was hype as things seemed to get a little louder as they patiently awaited the countdown. In unison everyone counted 10, 9, 8, 7, 6, 5, 4, 3, 2, 1 HAPPY NEWYEARS!!!!!! Dark brown, and cream colored confetti wafted through the air from above as the party seemed to have became more alive. All three floors were pumping from wall to wall as people drank, laughed, danced and got their mack on. In the mean time Cognac and her girls were standing around the table talking with Demarco and a couple of his boys. Demarco let everybody know that he was about to get them another round of Patron and turned around to get the attention of the waiter and place his order. Keith and a couple of his boys had walked up from the other side. Keith was buzzing and didn't notice that Cognac was talking to Demarco because he had walked away. Keith walked up to her, grabbed her hand, and started talking to her. Demarco turned around, caught off guard thinking to himself who the fuck is this dude just disrespecting him like that. Before Cognac could even get it out that she was there talking with Demarco for a moment, Demarco was already expressing himself defending his manhood.

"Damn nigga, you just gone disrespect me like that, my man?" Demarco said said with a slight scowl on his face.

"Nigga, what the fuck is you talking about? I'm here kicking it with her, brah! Don't come on me with that dumb shit!" Keith said with a pissed look on his face.

"Nigga, she here with me brah! That's what the fuck I'm talking about." Demarco said, mean mugging him seriously.

Demarco's boys, and Keith's boys were trying to sort of calm the drama down but was ready to scrap just in case the shit went down.

"Whack ass nigga's always wanna try to claim somebody that ain't claiming them! You better slow ya roll play boy. You don't know who you fucking with!" Keith said, ready to beat Demarco's ass.

"Bitch you don't know who you fucking with muthafucka! You better get the fuck on before you get chopped up and robbed, bitch!" Demarco said, ready for whatever.

The fellas were so loud that they never heard Cognac trying to peace out the situation. Regina and Benita grabbed their things and were looking around for Peaches. Regina called Peaches to find out where she was at but it kept going to her voicemail. Before anything could escalate security was there to break the shit up before a fight broke out. Cognac, Regina, and Benita walked outside to see if Peaches was out there and low and behold they found her across the street kissing Antonio. Peaches had just finished telling Antonio that she liked him but she just wasn't ready for a relationship, and wanted to take things slow, and Antonio had no problems with that. Peaches turned around when she heard Benita's loud voice, and her heels click clacking across the concrete.

"Girl, we got to go! Them nigga's was about to be fighting up in there." Benita said very animated, talking to Peaches.

"What?" Peaches asked, turning around wondering what the hell happened.

"We about to go. Both them dudes was trying to holla at Cognac at the same time and got in to it.

"What the fuck? Damn, these dudes be trippin." Antonio said as he walked them to their car.

Antonio saw them to their car safely and hooked back up with his boy Dennis and left. Club security escorted Keith and his boys out to assure the safety of the crowd so that the party could continue comfortably. Being that Demarco was one of the promoters they allowed him to stay seeing that security iced the situation before a fight broke out. Regina carefully drove up Woodward as the snow started coming down wetting the street.

"Damn girl, yo ass got dudes about to fight just to get that booty." Benita said, humorously.

"I don't know what be wrong with these dudes, they be trippin." Cognac stressed.

"Yeah but why it got to be the sexy looking dudes? Why can't it be the ugly ones that do that shit, that way it ain't got shit to do with us?" Peaches asked humorously.

"You are a fool with your silly ass." Cognac replied.

"I'm just playing, I don't want none of my brothas out here fighting and killing each other." Peaches added.

"That's for real, its time out for all that fighting and drama. These dudes is shooting now days, and I ain't trying to be a part of that mess." Regina concurred.

"Damn Coney, I know you glad you got up out of there before some stuff jumped off. Yo ass be meeting them dudes that be going nuts over you." Benita said.

"Well I'm just glad we got up out of there before the drama jumped off. I'm glad we on our way home safe and sound, and leaving all that mess behind us." Regina said as she looked at the flickering lights of the Fox Theatre as they rode by.

"Damn but that one dude was so nice. He had everything laid out, the steak, the lobster. That shit was good as hell." Peaches said giving her underlined remarks.

"Yeah, but that other guy dropped five bills on me with his number wrapped up in the middle about a week and a half ago at footlocker." Cognac highlighted.

"What?! Are you for real?" Peaches asked all animated.

"I'm so serious. He bought me a pair of shoes and inside was a five hundred dollars with his number wrapped up in it. I swear on everything." Cognac answered.

"Your ass always got it going on." Benita added.

"On some real talk I know them dudes are drug dealers and I know it feels good to have all that money spent on you, and taking you different places, but in the end it ain't nothing but problems and bad news. Besides you just got out of a relationship with one so I know you ain't trying to get back in that drama anyway." Regina said.

"I feel you...I feel you." Cognac said, shaking her head as they drove home.

21

Straight Up

So...I know y'all wondering what the hell is going on in my mind right now. These past two weeks have been major fuckin crazy. My girl fucked my man in MY muthafuckin bed, my man tells me he's married and then I find out I'm pregnant by this muthafucka! Then this nigga turn around and try to kill me. What the fuck?! That's some shit that will drive a woman crazy, and Y'all wonder why we be bitter, and nuttin up on Y'all asses. I ain't trying to say it's right that we be that way but hey, it is what it is. Now I got these two dudes I just met, Keith, and Demarco. I know them niggas is street niggas, and I know that them type of dudes will treat a girl good for the moment then turn around and treat the next chick the same way the next night. And just to keep it real, when we date these thugs and ballers and get hurt it ain't nobody else to blame but ourselves. All that blaming our fathers and mothers over and over for the fucked up dudes we choose to date is played out. If you're attracted to no good niggas, and then you get hurt by one, it's okay to say shame on them. If you turn around and date the same dude that hurt you or the same type of dude, treating you the same way and you get hurt again then its shame on you, flat the hell out. And I hear what my cousin Regina is saying about I don't need to fuck with nobody right now because I just got out of a fucked up relationship with a no good nigga, but...hey, I say let the chips fall where they may, and where ever that is, I don't give a fuck. I'll holla at Y'all sometimes this summer. Duces....

Also by Men-Tal
SALON TALK 2
187 Degrees of Danger

"Sneak Peek"

Passion and Flames

The repetitive sound of the headboard knocked against the wall every time Cedric stroked Cynthia's plump round ass, doggy-style. Damn, it ain't nothing like some good ass make up sex. Cynthia was a moaner especially whenever he'd hit that spot, and the sex faces she'd make made him want to fuck the shit out of her even harder. The flickering light from the candles highlighted the beautiful definition of her frame. She loved the way he pulled her hair, and every time he smacked her on the ass it would send erotic impulses to her vagina making her juices produce ridiculously.

"YES DADDY, GIVE IT TO ME HARDER BABY, FASTER! I love it when you give it to me Doggy-style, got damn!" Cynthia said intensely as she looked back at him.

Cedric got a good grip on her shoulder length hair with one hand and pulled as he continuously laid the wood to her like a reckless lumberjack. Cynthia was a freak who got off on ruff sex, and loved it when he called her names and choked her sometimes.

"I love it when you pull my fucking hair, Damn you're about to make me fucking cum!" Cynthia said loud as fuck as she clutched the bed sheets, stiffening her body, climaxing outrageously.

Cedric could feel her wetness all around his dick, trickling down his inner thighs. His pulse and breathing accelerated the more his cum built up ready to explode. The feeling grew more and more intense as he tried to get in as many strokes as he could. He stroked her more, and more till he could no longer hold back then pulled it out and jacked his cum all over her ass. Cynthia turned around and grabbed his dick, squeezing out the rest of his nut. She twirled her tongue around the head and then sucked it slow and passionately.

"I takes care of mines. Don't forget that shit." she said as she got up and walked into the bathroom to take a shower.

"I feel you, pumpkin. That shit was the bomb." Cedric replied.

He laid back on the bed, placing his hands behind his head thinking to himself how much he loved her. He couldn't wait to surprise her by proposing to her at the Chocolate and Cream Theme New Years Eve Ball to bring in 2011. He started getting sleepy and his eyelids were barely staying open. Just as he started drifting off he was alarmed as Cynthia's cell phone started vibrating. He was shocked that she had forgotten to take it with her into the bathroom like she normally does. He reached over, grabbed it and looked at the screen even more shocked that she had forgotten to put her security lock on. He felt like he couldn't look through it fast enough as he did his best to see all that he could see before she got out the shower and came back into the room. He found the evidence he was looking for when he saw that it read she had a video message from Damon. Fire immediately shot through his fucking veins as he thought to himself who the fuck is Damon! He clicked on the video and watched carefully. He didn't want to believe his eyes at first and peeped at the screen with his mouth open in disbelief. His heart pounded through his chest and his jaws tightened. Veins surfaced in his face as the whites of his eyes took a slight reddish tent. Enraged is just an understatement as of the way he felt when he saw that it was a video of Cynthia sucking the fuck out of Damon's dick. Damon was palming her head and stroking her face. Cedric felt like he had the wind knocked out of his chest with a sledge hammer, leaving him feeling empty inside. A text message appeared right after the video message which read "Hello baby. How is daddy's sweetheart doing? I'm missing you like crazy! When you gone cut that muthafucka Cedric loose and come be with the man you suppose to be fuckin with? Fuck that nigga." Cedric became so furiously heated that his ears began to burn. He walked over to the dresser, and grabbed the bottle of Moet and took a big gulp of it from the neck. He walked over to the closet and...............

Salon Talk – 187 Degrees of Danger coming this summer 2011.

Other Books By Men-Tal

SPIT- As if the pain was not enough...witnessing the murder

of his childhood peers and having his best friend, Diangelo take his last breath in his arms...As if the deception, controversy, relationship issues, nightlife and violence is not enough to make a good man loose his sanity and religion... sometimes the micro-phone and spotlight is a man's sanctuary and redemption...Life...is like a loaded gun pointed at your head leaving you with two options live or die and one question...What would you do?

Silent Screams is a collection of thought provoking poems that elaborate on the many aspects of our lives ranging from love, relationships, intimacy, and much more.

SPIT and Silent Screams are available for purchase on your major online book sites

Contact Information Page

Men-Tal

Novelist/ Poet/ Art Illustrator
CEO of Essential Expressions
Wordsmith for personalized cards
For Birthdays, Holidays Greetings, Weddings
Baby Showers, Just because, Condolence etc.

WritingExtraordinaire@yahoo.com

Gentle Touch Phlebotomy Education, LLC

Chantelle R. White CEO/ Director/ Instructor
23300 Greenfield RD Suite 212
Oak Park MI, 48237
Gentletouch.org
"Where drawing blood is more than a skill it's an art"
"We're changing lives one blood draw at a time"

AIM- All In Mind Designs

Maurice Ingram
Graphics Designer/ Art Illustrator
Hanufel8@yahoo.com

D&E Photography
Darius Blackmon
Graphic Designer
(313)-734-2005

Awesome Cuts
15300 W. McNichols
Detroit MI, 48235
Ms. Que (Hair Stylist)

www.ingramcontent.com/pod-product-compliance
Lightning Source LLC
Chambersburg PA
CBHW050519260626
47157CB00004B/1392